Gefilte Fish

in the House of Bedlam

Larry Baumhor

To Cornelia, a customer at the garage, who has shared her literary adventures allowing me to peek into her past and live vicariously. If I took you with me we would have found Salinger a lot faster.

Enjoy!

Larry Baumhor

Copyright © 2008 by Larry Baumhor

All rights reserved. No part of this publication may be reproduced, distributed, or transmitted in any form or by any means, electronic or mechanical, including photocopying, recording, or by any information storage and retrieval system, without written permission from the author.

Larry Baumhor, Publisher
Web site at www.shortstoriesandphotos.com

First Edition, September 2008

Senior Editor
Brad Dasher

Editing Consultant
Joel Rotenberg

Editor
Larry Baumhor

Cover Design and Production
Joel Rotenberg
Ken Brown

Design and Layout
Steve Rydzewski

Printer and Binder
King Printing
Tom Campbell

Cover by Francisco Jose de Goya y Lucientes
The Sleep of Reason Produces Monsters
Philadelphia Museum of Art: Purchased with the SmithKline Beckman Corporation Fund, 1949

Printed in the United States of America

For my son, Andrew

Contents

Looking for Mr. Salinger	3
The House of Bedlam	20
Livin' and Lovin' in a Reverie	35
Pick your Nose in New York	53
The Bizzaro World	56
Our Western World	63
Poems for Strippers	70
Children of Baseball	77
Gefilte Fish	86
Your Disco Buddy	97
So Your Kid Wants to be a Sportscaster	102

Acknowledgements

With no prior editing experience, I assumed this would be the least of my problems. However, the editing became the most difficult and tedious task in producing this book. And quite frankly, I despise it. Writing and rewrites are my passion; editing almost sent me to the House of Bedlam. Salute to the editors of the world! It seemed that there was no end in sight, as I wanted this project to be the best it could be. Besides the obvious, such as the use of commas, quotations within quotations, the use of italics etc., the tweaking of words became my nemesis. Where should I stop, and when should I stop making changes, as small as they were? I finally, after near exhaustion, felt comfortable with the finished stories. I could easily see how the editor writer relationship can become strained. Thank goodness I have been friends with Brad Dasher for 32 years and our disagreements were not taken personally, and were appreciated. I wanted to maintain a certain rhythm in my dialogue and narrative with my own brand of nuances, and I accomplished this without compromise. Brad, who is a renaissance man, with experience as a standup comic and editor was passionate, helpful, and was a major influence in the editing of *Gefilte Fish in the House of Bedlam*.

Joel Rotenberg, who I'm friendly with from the Garage Antique Flea Market in New York, is a writer and translator of books in German and French. When I first began consulting with Joel about my project, I'm certain he had no idea it would turn into weeks of up to fifteen emails a day of grammar, punctuation, cover design, and formatting text questions. The more I felt I was imposing on Joel, his patience, passion, and concern reassured me of his commitment. Joel's command of the English language and Yiddish translations resolved many editing questions. After informing Joel of the title of my book, and expressing my desire for a torturous, humorous cover, Joel designed the cover of *Gefilte Fish in the House of Bedlam.* Joel, who has angelic like qualities, perhaps was sent from heaven to help me.

Ken Brown is also a friend from the Garage Antique Flea Market in New York. Ken is an artist, illustrator, and photographer. He began his artistic endeavor creating light shows for many of the big-name rock bands of the 1960s in the Boston, MA area. His photography has won awards, his art has been published, and he also illustrates book covers. Ken also created his own line of postcards and greeting cards. When I informed Ken of my project, he immediately offered his years of professional experience, and for this I am extremely fortunate and grateful. Like all artists, Ken has his quirks. He rejected over one hundred photos of gefilte fish for the cover. "It's not appropriate to use paper plates for the gefilte fish. They don't serve Passover dinners like that, and the carrots and fish don't look good," Ken said. Now, I'm dealing with a gefilte fish connoisseur, I thought. And to top it off, he's not even Jewish. "Ken," I said, "my grandmother served gefilte fish with cigarette ashes on the top. Don't worry about the paper plate, I just want the cover to have a strong aesthetic appeal and pop out at you," Finally, we had our gefilte fish, and Ken was able to work with Joel's concept to create a vision that I desired for my book cover.

If I wasn't ending up in The House of Bedlam from the editing, I surely would get there from the design and layout of my text. Tasks of technical and tedious projects often cause me to act like a madman having convulsions. I was dealing with both while producing *Gefilte Fish in the House of Bedlam*. I became ill, ranting, raving, crying, and screaming. "Save me from this misery," I screamed. I had to format the entire book in Microsoft Word and then transfer it to a PDF file. The only experience I had with Microsoft Word was double space and spell check. Now I was dealing with the font style and size, leading, margins, headers, footers, hyphens, justification, and more. When I would hit one command, something in the text would get fucked-up. When I justified then there was too much word spacing in a sentence. Staples offers a consulting program for Microsoft Word. They refunded my fifty dollars. "It's too complicated," they said. I called my friend Steve Rydzewski, a graphic designer, who works with an Apple computer, and uses Quark and InDesign. Steve, who works in advertising, doesn't get home until 9 P.M. At first he refused, saying, "I'm exhausted and know nothing about Microsoft Word." I broke down and cried, literally in desperation. On many nights, Steve came over and worked with me until the wee hours of the morning, resolving the design and layout of *Gefilte Fish in the House of Bedlam*. You should try this crying stuff, it really works. Thank you Steve!

Men cannot have babies. But they can give birth to books. My obstetrician, Dr. Tom Campbell, from King Printing, delivered my baby, *Gefilte Fish in the House of Bedlam.* I was very neurotic, and this being my first delivery, intensified my neurosis. There were several false alarms, at eight centimeters dilated and contractions every five minutes, I thought I was ready to deliver. "Not so," said Dr. Campbell. And then I went through a stage of hysterics, caused by excessive editing, and the inability to format the text to Dr. Campbell's requirements. Dr. Campbell's knowledge, reassurance and patience helped me through the most severe labor pains one could only imagine. Thank you Dr. Campbell!

To my dearest friend, Harris Kramer, who has read my manuscripts-the good, bad, and ugly-for over fifteen years, and has endured many dinners of self-loathing and kvetching. Here's to you my friend. We made it!

I would be remiss, if I didn't mention my friends from the Antique Garage Flea Market in New York where I sell vintage photos. The Garage is closing sometime in 2009, ending an era of antique flea markets in Chelsea. Many of my friends affiliated with this market are artists, illustrators, photographers, writers, and decorators who inspired and encouraged my writing and publication of *Gefilte Fish in the House of Bedlam.* We have all been bound by the love of photography, but it's our relationships that will live on, hopefully in person, and if not in memory. Surrounding yourself with creative people fosters an inspirational environment and mindset to create. And for this I am grateful.

Quotes from other Artists

(1) "Blowin' in the Wind," written by Bob Dylan, released 1963 album, *The Freewheelin Bob Dylan*. Quoted in "Livin' and Lovin' in a Reverie."
(2) "Homeward Bound," written by Paul Simon, 1966. Quoted in "Livin' and Lovin' in a Reverie."
(3) "Stuck Inside of Mobile with the Memphis Blues Again," written by Bob Dylan, 1966 album *Blonde on Blonde*. Quoted in "Livin' and Lovin' in a Reverie."
(4) "For Once in My Life," written by Ron Miller and Orlando Murden for Motown Records, Jobete Publishing Company in 1967. Quoted in "Livin' and Lovin' in a Reverie."
(5) "Get Me to the Church on Time," composed by Frederick Loewe, lyrics by Alan Jay, for the 1956 musical My Fair Lady. Quoted in "Livin' and Lovin' in a Reverie."

(1) Mighty Mouse Theme Song, The lyrics to the "Mighty Mouse Playhouse," 1955 CBS TV Network, original created for theatrical presentation by Paul Terry's Terry-toons since 1942, music by Philip A. Scheib, lyrics by Marshall Barer. Quoted in "So Your Kid Wants to be a Sportscaster."
(2) "Beauty and the Beast," music by Alan Menken, lyrics by Howard Ashman, 1991. Quoted in "So Your Kid Wants to be a Sportscaster."

(3) "Baby Face," lyrics by Benny Davis, music by Harry Akst, 1926. Quoted in "So Your Kid Wants to be a Sportscaster."

(4) "Carolina in My Mind," written by James Taylor, 1968. Quoted in "So Your Kid Wants to be a Sportscaster."

(5) Addams Family Theme Song, lyrics by Vic Mizzy, 1964. Quoted in "So Your Kid Wants to be a Sportscaster."

(6) "Who's on First?" by William Bud Abbott and Lou Costello. Quoted in "So Your Kid Wants to be a Sportscaster."

Dear Readers,

My eleven short stories are a labor of love that began twenty-one years ago when I penned my first story. To say the least, it sucked. But I fell in love with writing, and continued to pursue my dream. I sharpened my skills, writing novels, a nonfiction manuscript, articles, letters, poems, and short stories. I began to accumulate rejections. I marched on, in pursuit of becoming the first published author in my family. I accumulated more rejections. As my life twisted and turned, my writing followed this journey, observing and documenting the disturbances, nuances, epiphanies, and fantasies that were exclusively mine. I accumulated more rejections.

A funny thing happened on the way to self-publishing *Gefilte Fish in the House of Bedlam*: my reality and fantasy of thoughts and events became intermingled. Did these events and feelings I was writing about really happen the way I described them in my stories? Are you able to speak to someone and convey the exact truth of your story, or are there nuances, embellishments, and interpretations of your story? What was fiction and what was nonfiction in my writing became more difficult to separate. Some of the stories you'll read are fiction, some are nonfiction, and some are fiction but mostly nonfiction. As fiction and nonfiction became blurred, I was intrigued, and decided to become a real character in my stories.

Larry Baumhor

Gefilte Fish in the House of Bedlam

Looking for Mr. Salinger

As I was driving to Cornish, New Hampshire to speak with Mr. Salinger my motives became more clear, I was bullshitting myself. Yes, I am writing a short story on this experience, and I would like his advice on my twenty years of unpublished literary material, and yes, I want Mr. Salinger's insights into my psychological conflict of self-publishing on the Internet. But in part, and perhaps in large part, I desired something Mr. Salinger avoided for over 40 years as a recluse: notoriety. I'm a phony. I'm driven by ulterior motives. Though I don't know of anybody that's not a phony, at times, when desiring something. Being a hypocrite is not black and white, but rather shaded in layers of complex nuances, some acceptable, others illegal, immoral, repulsive, and even murderous. Nevertheless, I was in pursuit of notoriety, and was attempting to use Mr. Salinger to achieve my goal.

This was a well thought out plan on my part. I have OCD and was determined not to leave Cornish under any circumstances until I spoke with Mr. Salinger. The fact he was 89 years old, probably declining in health, and doesn't speak to anyone publicly, made no difference. I was on a mission, and like a Boy Scout I needed equipment. I printed t-shirts that read: Looking For Mr. Salinger-on the front-To Discuss My 20 Years Of Unpublished Fiction And My Conflict Of Internet Publishing-on the back. I made placards and a sandwich board with the same information as the t-shirts. I printed a business card with the same information, including my cell phone number. I purchased a bullhorn. I was prepared to battle the authorities, the townspeople, and an old dying literary icon, just to get my story. However, the most important thing I had going for me was not my persistence, obsession, nor my equipment; it was my gift of gab, my personality, my charm, my ability to adlib and persuade that I would depend on, and ultimately these were my weapons of resistance.

It was Monday morning, May 12th, 2008, when I arrived at The Chase House Bed and Breakfast Inn of Cornish, New Hampshire. The 160 acre estate with a 1766 Settlement Colony-style house, located on the banks of the Connecticut River, offers a spellbinding view of Vermont's Mount Ascutney. I was wearing my t-shirt and baseball cap that said Looking For Mr. Salinger. I knew I was going to be stared at like some kind of freak, and this was ok, this was my intent. "Hi, my name is Larry Baumhor. I have a reservation."

"Madge Kramer, nice to meet you."

"I'm at a loss for words as to the charm and beauty of your facility. This is truly a surreal paradise. I'm a history buff and would love to know where I can get some information, perhaps a book or brochures on the Inn and surrounding areas."

"The Inn is a National Historic Landmark and a Colonial settlement. Perhaps you'll find some information in our gift shop, if not I recommend Violet's Book Exchange in Claremont."

"How far is Claremont from here?"

"About 10 miles."

"How about restaurants in the area?"

"Here's a brochure with some attractions and restaurants. I highly recommend Windsor Station Restaurant. The food is great, and if you like history the restaurant was built in 1900, and was a passenger and freight depot. They restored it in 1977. The likes of Calvin Coolidge and Teddy Roosevelt have passed through. It's in Windsor Vermont, but only 4 miles from here."

"I'll try it tonight. I'm sure you've noticed my t-shirt and hat. The main reason I've come to Cornish is to speak with Mr. Salinger. I earn a living selling vintage photos, but my real passion is writing. I've been at it for 20 years, 6 manuscript books, over 20 short stories, hundreds of letters and poems, but nothing really published. I wanted to ask Mr. Salinger his advice on writing, and now I'm thinking of self-publishing on the internet, but I am in conflict about this method. I know Mr. Salinger is a very private man and is up there in age, and therefore if I don't get a chance to meet him that's ok, but at least I know I've tried. I wanted to give Mr. Salinger one of my short stories, 'Gefilte Fish.' Do you know how I can get in touch with him?"

"I can't begin to tell you how many people have come through looking for Mr. Salinger. I'm sorry, I do not have any information on Mr. Salinger or his whereabouts, though he does patronize establishments in the area including the Windsor Station Restaurant. What is 'Gefilte Fish'?"

"'Gefilte Fish' is a humorous psychological short story about Passover dinners at my Grandparents. Please forgive me if I'm presumptuously imposing, but here's 'Gefilte Fish' with my card and cell phone. If you happen to know anybody who knows somebody that knows Mr. Salinger, please ask them to give him 'Gefilte Fish' and my card. Again, I apologize, but I made a promise to myself that I would at least try to speak with Mr. Salinger. Thank you very much. I appreciate it."

I decided to take a ride into Claremont, New Hampshire and visit Violet's Book Exchange. What else would Mr. Salinger patronize if not a book store, I thought. I'll find him, you'll see. Located at 28 Opera House Square, a quaint little shop with walls of used books, specializing in literature and history. I introduced myself to the owner Martha, an attractive hippie looking woman in her fifties. After exchanging small talk and telling her about my vintage photo business, there was an immediate connection. Martha collected vintage snapshots, and particularly photo-booth and arcade type snapshots.

"Here's my vintage photo business card. When you come to New York, stop by the Chelsea Antique Garage. Come to my booth and I'll take care of you. I have thousands of photos for you to look at and plenty of photobooth and arcade photos. I can even scan a few and I'll e-mail them to you. If they're appealing, you can purchase them."

Her dark eyes gleamed with joy. "Thank you, I've heard so much about the Chelsea Antique Garage. Now that I know you, I'll come visit you this summer." We both liked the Beat writers and Henry Miller. I found a kindred spirit, and I saw no rings on her fingers, but I was scared to ask if she was single.

"The real reason I came to Cornish, New Hampshire-I'm staying at the Chase House Bed and Breakfast Inn- is to speak with Mr. Salinger." The gleam in her eyes went dark-her infectious smile disappeared, and her face became tight with angst. I just ruined whatever credibility I built during my two hours in the store. *What a putz,* I thought.

"I know this seems weird, and it's an infringement on Mr. Salinger's privacy, but I promised myself I would try. I have tons of unpublished books, stories, letters, and essays. For twenty years I've been rejected, and now I'm thinking of self publishing on the Internet. I wanted to ask Mr. Salinger his opinion of my work, and the conflict I'm having about publishing on the Internet. I don't even want to know if you know Mr. Salinger, or if in fact he comes into your store, but please, if you know anybody that knows him, give him my 'Gefilte Fish' short story and card with my cell phone. I know we hit it off and you seem really nice. I have to be honest with you, I'm a phony. I'm writing a short story about this experience and would only be using Mr. Salinger to gain notoriety." I handed Martha my short story and Looking For Mr. Salinger card and left the store.

Cornish is a small rural town with very few stores and a population of 1,661. If you wanted to go to a bigger town with stores and a Main St., you had to either cross the Cornish-Windsor Covered Bridge into Windsor, Vermont, or drive to Claremont, New Hampshire about nine miles from Cornish. Many local residents living in Cornish shopped in Windsor and Claremont. I went back to my car and put on my wooden Looking For Mr. Salinger sandwich board. In one hand I held my bullhorn, and in the other were copies of "Gefilte Fish" with my card stapled at the top left corner. I began walking down Main Street in Claremont. I pushed the button on the bullhorn and began speaking: "Good afternoon residents of Sullivan County, my name is Larry Baumhor and I'm looking for Mr. Salinger. I am a frustrated unpublished author of twenty years. I would like someone to please give Mr. Salinger my short story 'Gefilte Fish.'" I began handing out "Gefilte Fish" as though it was a manifesto, a document that would break down the barriers of genre literature. "Please take 'Gefilte Fish' and give it to Mr. Salinger," I yelled into the bullhorn.

I stopped in every store on Main Street and handed out "Gefilte Fish." I began to speak again into the bullhorn, "I'm looking for Mr. Salinger," when I heard a siren and then a sheriff pulled over and double parked on Main Street.

"What are you doing?" asked Sheriff Warren.

"I'm looking for Mr. Salinger."

"You're in violation of section 16.05.12 of the Sullivan County Ordinance: No person shall disturb the peace, quiet and comfort of any neighborhood by creating any disturbing or unreasonably loud noise."

"I'm sorry officer, I'm just trying to get the word out to Mr. Salinger and give him a copy of my short story, 'Gefilte Fish.'" I thought I had the right to freedom of speech?"

"You are disturbing the peace. I'm giving you a citation for $100.00. You're going to have to stop this. And Mr. Salinger is a private man who does not want to be bothered with this nonsense."

Things didn't go too well in Claremont, except I really liked Martha, but I'm sure once she found out about my buffoonery, I didn't have a chance in hell. I must have spoken to over one hundred people. These towns are small, someone must know Mr. Salinger or at least know where he lives. I went back to the Inn, showered and headed over the bridge to the Windsor Station Restaurant in Vermont. I gave "Gefilte Fish" to the hostess, waitress, and busboy. After dinner, I walked around town handing out my manifesto. I engaged in conversation with anyone willing to talk to me. At this point I was getting venomous stares and cold responses. Some people walked across the street deliberately to avoid me. In one day I became ostracized. One lady grabbed hold of "Gefilte Fish," threw it down on the ground and said, "Get out of this community, stop bothering us. You're a kook."

I dejectedly and exhaustedly drove back to the Inn.

The next morning, I drove to the post office on route 120 in Cornish, thinking someone would at least give a copy of "Gefilte Fish" to Mr. Salinger. No luck, they refused to give me any information, nor would they accept any copies of "Gefilte Fish." I drove along Route 120 until I got to the Cornish General Store, and that's where I met Billy Smithson, a 78 year old Cornish bred and raised New Hampshirian.

"No one likes me around here, Mr. Smithson. They think I'm disturbing the peace and trying to bother Mr. Salinger. He probably comes in here, right?"

"Every now and then, he used to come in a lot. I know J.D. from when he first moved here in the 50s. He ain't nothin' to me, as long as you don't talk to him about personal stuff or that writing of his, he's a nice guy."

"Would it be a terrible inconvenience if I left you my short story and card with my cell phone to give to him."

"What you want to do that for, he lives right up at that road," as he directs me with his finger. "J.D. lives in the brown hilltop chalet with a sun deck facing the Connecticut River. You can't miss it."

"I can't thank you enough Mr. Smithson. Thank you so much. I appreciate it." I went right to the house Mr. Smithson described, except there was nothing on the mailbox and not even an address number on the street or any of the doors. It was a simple home, but the view was spectacular. I got out of the car and walked up to the door with "Gefilte Fish" in my hand. My heart was pounding. Was I here? Was this really Mr. Salinger's house? There was no bell. I knocked, lightly at first, and waited one minute. I knocked harder and waited two minutes. I knocked a third time and a fourth time, no answer. I'll go back to the Inn and come back after dinner, surely someone, if not Mr. Salinger, would be home. Still, no one answered after supper. I'll try early in the morning. Tomorrow, I thought for sure, I would get Mr. Salinger in the morning.

That night, I wrote a letter to Mr. Salinger that I was going to leave in his mail box, with a copy of "Gefilte Fish" and my card.

Dear Mr. Salinger:

My passion has been writing for the past twenty years. Despite the frustration of 6 unpublished books, over 20 short stories, hundreds of poems, letters, and essays, I continue to dream. Though at 54 years of age, one must wonder, if perhaps, I'm just not good enough. I drove up here with the intent of handing you my short story "Gefilte Fish," and asking your opinion (I brought other stories with me too) on both my writing and my conflict of self-publishing on the Internet. I write self-confessional fiction in the first person, and I'm not sure if I want to expose myself to the world. And I also feel that the Internet is a second-rate form of publishing. I'm a purist and want my words in a book. I'm selling out.

Driving up here to Cornish, I had an epiphany, realizing I was bullshitting myself in that I wanted to use you for the sole purpose of notoriety while I write this short story about our meeting. I'm a hypocrite, pretending to ask for your advice, not that I don't want it, but your name and interview would mean more. I'm ashamed of myself. Perhaps this whole thing is lunacy on my part. During one thought I think it is lunacy and then I have another thought that says I'll do anything to get published. It's an act of desperation for sure, and for this I'm sorry.

                        Sincerely,

                        Larry Baumhor

At 8:00 AM, I knocked on Mr. Salinger's door, and knocked again and again and again, but no answer. I left the letter, the short story, and my card in his mail box. I drove to Route 120 and Cornish Stage Road, parked my car, and got out with my placard, some "Gefilte Fish" stories, and my bullhorn. I began holding the placard Looking For Mr. Salinger, and as the cars stopped at the intersection, I handed out "Gefilte Fish" stories. After an hour and a half I was getting bored, so I picked up the bullhorn: "Mr. Salinger, I'm looking for you, please come out wherever you are. Does anyone know where I can give Mr. Salinger my short story?"

Within twenty minutes I heard a siren. It was Sheriff Warren again and he didn't look too happy. "You're under arrest," said the Sheriff in an authoritative tone, "for disturbing the peace and stalking Mr. Salinger."

"You've got to be kidding. I never threatened Mr. Salinger. I've never stalked him or threatened him. I haven't even seen him." I was handcuffed and placed in the back seat of the sheriff's car. I was driven to the police department and placed in a holding cell for two and a half hours, and then driven to the Claremont

District Court in Claremont, New Hampshire. The court has jurisdiction over the city of Claremont and the town of Cornish.

"All rise, the Honorable Judge Ken Jones Presiding."

"Do you Larry Baumhor, solemnly swear to tell the truth, the whole truth, and nothing but the truth, so help you God?"

"Yes, I do."

"Mr. Baumhor, on Monday May 12, 2008, in Claremont New Hampshire, you were given a citation for violating section 16.05.12 of the Claremont, New Hampshire Ordinance that states: No person shall disturb the peace, quiet, and comfort of any neighborhood by creating any disturbing or unreasonably loud noise. Is this correct Mr. Baumhor?"

"Yes Your Honor that is correct, however, I will be appealing this citation on the grounds it is ill-defined, with no guidelines for what is unreasonably loud noise, and furthermore it violates my First Amendment of freedom of speech."

"That certainly is your right, Mr. Baumhor. However, today, May 14, 2008, you once again violated this ordinance by using your bullhorn on Route 120 and Cornish Stage Road in Cornish, New Hampshire. And that's when Mr. Warren arrested you. "Is that correct?"

"Yes, Your Honor, I did use the bullhorn today."

"Until you, Mr. Baumhor, who lives out of state, repeals this ordinance, you're under my jurisdiction. Do you understand?"

"Yes, Your Honor."

"What was going through your mind when you decided to use the bullhorn again after getting a citation?"

"I don't know Your Honor. I'm sorry, it won't happen again. I have OCD and I've been obsessed with finding Mr. Salinger and giving him my short story to read."

"How many times did you go to Mr. Salinger's house and knock on his door?

"Three times."

"How many different days?"

"Two different days. Twice yesterday and once today."

"Have you ever been diagnosed with any psychiatric disorders?"

"Yes, I have OCD, depression and anxiety, and a low self esteem."

"Do you take any medicine?"

"No, I used to but I haven't taken it in years."

"Have you ever been hospitalized for mental illness?"

"No."

"I'm ordering a full psychiatric evaluation for you. I am issuing a restraining order against you, where you are not to go within 100 yards of Mr. Salinger's house. Do I make myself clear? If you violate this order, you could be charged with stalking, and face up to five years in prison. My suggestion is that you stop looking for Mr. Salinger and go home to Philadelphia."

"Your Honor, I want him to read my short story and ask Mr. Salinger a couple of questions about my writing and the possibility of Internet publishing."

"I've been on this bench for twenty six years and I've never had so many complaints in such a short time about one person. You have inundated every store and every nook and cranny of Cornish and Claremont with 'Gefilte Fish.' It was also brought to my attention that you flooded Windsor, Vermont with 'Gefilte Fish.' And if that's not bad enough, is it true that you also went into residential areas in Claremont and Cornish and placed 'Gefilte Fish' in mail boxes?"

"Yes, I did Your Honor."

"How many 'Gefilte Fish' stories have you given out during the past three days?"

"I'm not sure, but I would say over one thousand."

"I'm going to read the first sentence of 'Gefilte Fish' for the record, and then ask you if this story is yours. Have you ever eaten smoked gefilte fish, not with the traditional horseradish, but with a couple of cigarette ashes on top, billows of cigarette smoke in the air, served by a Jewish Grandmother who wore a brassiere as a blouse, with a Viceroy cigarette dangling from her lips?" A lot of people in the court room laughed when they heard the first sentence of "Gefilte Fish."

"Approach the bench Mr. Baumhor." Is this a copy of your story 'Gefilte Fish' that you handed out over one thousand copies to the residents in Sullivan County, New Hampshire?"

"Yes, Your Honor, that's my 'Gefilte Fish' story."

"Duly noted, marked Exhibit "A" and entered into the record. Is this your card, Looking For Mr. Salinger, that you attached to 'Gefilte Fish' and handed out over one thousand copies to the residents of Sullivan County, New Hampshire?"

"Yes, Your Honor it is."

"Marked Exhibit "B" and entered into the record. Please take a look at this sandwich board, placard, t-shirt, and hat and identify them."

"They are all mine Your Honor."

"They will be entered into the record as evidence. Do you have any other questions before I close this proceeding?"

"May I make a statement to the court?"

"Go ahead."

"I would like to extend my deep appreciation and gratitude to a most gracious hospitable community that welcomed me for the most part, despite my attempt to meet Mr. Salinger. And for those of you who I have offended, annoyed or aggravated, I want to extend my heartfelt apologies, as this was not my intent. Out of my desperation to get published, I perhaps crossed the line of appropriate, socially acceptable behavior, and for this I am sorry. And I apologize to the court and to the Sheriff's Department for taking up their valuable time and the use of taxpayers' money."

I drove to Violet's Book Exchange to say goodbye to Martha. *You better get a hold of your life. What are you doing? You're a loser. You've isolated yourself from all your friends and family. You sit in that apartment day and night writing stories and living in fantasies. The only time you go out is to an occasional movie and book store or to buy and sell those stupid old photos. You haven't dated in years.* You know, you're right, I am a loser with a capital L. It was over, my quest, my obsession, it all turned into a failure.

"Hi Martha. I just got out of court and Judge Jones issued me a restraining order to stay 100 yards away from Mr. Salinger's house."

"Yeah, I know, it was on the radio, probably the TV too. You didn't see the reporters?"

"No, I was so out of it, I didn't know who was there. Although somebody did take a couple of pictures."

"I want you to come here tomorrow at 11:00 A.M. Mr. Salinger is coming here to meet with you."

"You're kidding me, right?"

"No, I'm dead serious. Don't ask me any questions. I'm not answering them. You come here tomorrow at 11:00, and I guarantee you Mr. Salinger will be here to talk with you."

"I'm sorry, this is overwhelming," as I broke down and cried, I hugged Martha. "I don't know how to thank you. I made a fool of myself. And this is what you do for me. I can't begin to tell you how much this means. I'm eternally grateful. Thank you."

"I'll see you tomorrow at 11:00 A.M."

I went back to the Inn and laid in bed all night, unable to close my eyes. What in God's name am I going to ask Mr. Salinger? I thought. Finally, I decided not to ask him anything about his personal life and his writings. I would ask him about my writings and give him other stories to read.

At 10:30, I arrived at Violet's Book Exchange. I looked around and only saw Martha.

"You look very nervous, just calm down," Martha said.

"Ok."

"He's just an ordinary person, a real nice guy."

"Ok."

At 10:45, Martha walked me in the back room, and sat me down at the table. It was a very tiny 7 by 7 room where Martha held books for customers, and there was a counter with a small refrigerator, a microwave, and coffee machine. "You sit at this table and at 11:00 Mr. Salinger will come through the back door and talk to you. I'm going up front, and I'm going to put a sign on the front door that I'll reopen at 12:00. I will be in the front of the store. I will not be back here with you. Are you ok? You don't look good."

"I didn't get any sleep last night. I'll be alright."

10:55 A.M., no Mr. Salinger, 10:58, no Mr. Salinger, 11:00, no Mr. Salinger, 11:02, no Mr. Salinger. At 11:04, the back door opened and in walked Mr. Salinger with a man and a woman by his side. His hair was grey but thick, his face wrinkled, and he walked with a cane. I felt Moses just parted the Red Sea. I was so nervous that in my mind I thought he really was Moses. I immediately stood up and said, "It's a pleasure to meet you." Mr. Salinger signaled me with both hands to sit down. The man and woman were standing. Mr. Salinger sat down at the table. It seemed like we were staring at each other for a while. "Thank you so much for meeting with me Mr. Salinger. It's quite an honor."

He placed his finger up to his lip to stop me from talking. "Martha has the information on my literary agent. You mail your stories there. I liked 'Gefilte

Fish.'" Mr. Salinger stood up, and as fast as you could say gefilte fish he was gone.

I drove back to Philadelphia and as soon as I opened my car door the paparazzi and TV cameras were in my face. Flash bulbs going off, lights in my eyes, mikes in my face, and questions flying at me. "What is Mr. Salinger like? How's his health? How long did you meet with him? Will he ever speak to the press? Is he writing? Is he going to publish? Will he publish posthumously? What did he say?"

"I can't answer these questions, because you'll read about it in my short story, 'Looking for Mr. Salinger.'

The House of Bedlam

As a result of my mental illness I checked myself into the House of Bedlam-known to all sane mortals as Psychiatric Central. My attorney advised me to use fictitious names, thus avoiding any libel or slander suits until the pending litigation is settled. Shortly after being discharged from Psychiatric Central, I was hit with a law suit. When one is sued one counters with a suit. More on this later. There are beds available at Psychiatric Central for those comrades who are dysfunctional, distressed, and/or unable to function within the rules laid down by society. If you're psychotic, depressed, or suffering from any of the Diagnostic and Statistical Manual of Mental Disorders, you too may be eligible for a bed. Everything seems to revolve around a bed. Eighty two beds minus twelve vacancies equals sixty occupied beds with an operating loss of two hundred and twenty five dollars per bed each day. However, only seventy three occupied beds are needed for matching funds from the state. Confusing? Don't worry about it. Just remember you're nothing more than a bed worth two hundred and twenty five dollars per day.

I drove through the masonry arches as the thumping of my tires on the cobblestones shimmed my wheels. I glanced over at the duck pond and saw two ducks bob underneath the water, probably to escape the fumes my 1980 Dodge Duster was emitting. Not a bad place, I thought to myself, for a little R & R. Look at the placement of the angular curved stones, as though they were cut in a miter box. At the age of forty, I now viewed things through an aesthetic eye. It was pleasure I sought, whether it be through a word, painting, sculpture, or stone. When not having nightmares, or having to face reality, I often find myself in a state of reverie, inside words dreaming of images. A house was no longer a house. A book was no longer a book. A woman was no longer a woman. Whatever wasn't art seemed to have no value to me. You'll have to put up with these digressions, if of course, you want to hear my story. Throughout life, one doesn't wander down a straight path without changing courses and getting flung on one's keister. So why should I put forth chronology, when chaos, its antitheses, is the order of life?

At any rate, it appeared I was in a palatial estate, with tree covered, winding cobblestone roads, a duck pond, a ball field, tennis courts, and even a walking path for those interested in escaping the House of Bedlam. There were three buildings, each housing patients, referred to as units A, B, and C. I was housed in unit B, bed 26. I referred to the units as wards, and the beds as bedlams. For three weeks I was ward B, bedlam 26.

Janice, my intake worker, a recent graduate with a masters in psychology, was a stunning blond, tall, with striking features. "Mr. Baumhor, will you fill out this evaluation form and then I have some questions for you."

"Ok."

"Mr. Baumhor, I see here you didn't put a phone number down."

"At times I prefer to live in isolation and come to terms with my psyche, but my phone was disconnected."

"What seems to be your problem?"

You're incredible. I'd marry you. I was sitting in front of Janice's desk, and as she sat there interviewing me I became mesmerized by her aura. Her skirt seemed to squeeze her legs together which didn't help matters. "I've been depressed."

"How long has your depression been going on?"

"My entire adult life."

"What symptoms do you experience when depressed?"

"I feel like a spider trapped in its own web."

"Have you ever been in therapy?"

My poetry for you would turn into an aphrodisiac. "Years ago in my late twenties I was in therapy with a few different therapists for about a year and a half."

"Are you taking any medication?"

If I could only feed you. "No."

"Why did you wait so long to seek therapy again?"

My hands feel the movement of your hips as we tango. "Because I'm happy."

"You're happy?"

"Yes, I have this creative energy that simultaneously destroys." *I would destroy you.* "In order to create or love one must destroy previous forms, transcend the norm. I destroy my son with love and I destroy myself in poetry."

"Do you have any irregular sleeping patterns?"

"Yes, my rem sleep seems to be in excess."

"What do you mean?"

Could you imagine if we were on an island together? "I live in my dreams about eighteen hours a day."

"Any problems with weight?"

I'd work out every day if I had you. "Yes, I could fluctuate fifty pounds depending if I'm destroying or creating."

"Do you have many friends?"

"Once a friend, tomorrow a foe. What's the difference?"

"Do you experience any visual or auditory hallucinations?"

I see you in panties and a bra. "I speak to dead poets and writers-Whitman, Miller, Poe, Plath, Eliot, Cummings, Dickinson."

"Do you see any flashes or trails?"

"No."

"Do you take any drugs?"

"Words are my drugs."

"Are you suicidal?"

"Death is always on my mind. I write about it and breathe it in as oxygen, but I have been unable to conquer it."

"Do you feel you can harm other people?"

"The structure of conspiratorial institutions harm people."

"So you feel there is a conspiracy to get you?"

"Yes, you yourself are in collusion."

"How's that?"

"You work for this institution, don't you?"

"According to your application, your occupation is a poet?"

"Yes."

"Do you earn money from this?"

"Yes, the state supports my art. Welfare pays my son and I to produce poetry. Can you imagine a nine year old Jew on welfare?"

"What's your insurance company?"

"Medical Assistance." I couldn't believe it. It was as simple as that. Based on the interview with Janice, I was an inmate in the House of Bedlam with Janice as my gatekeeper.

I was exhausted that first night, but I couldn't fall asleep. Although I had my own room and the bed was comfortable, there was a howling sound piercing the halls which seemed to reverberate in my head. I began to walk the halls and discovered shrieking sounds emanating from three rooms. I opened the door to my neighbor's lair and began howling.

"You wanna howl you crazy bastard, then I'm gonna howl with you." The howling stopped after I harmonized with my other two roommates and finally I was able to fall asleep.

In the morning I had my first session with Dr. Linton, who happened to be the chief psychiatrist on staff. I shook his hand with some trepidation, but overall it was an auspicious debut. Dr. Linton, a good looking man in his early fifties, sported a golden tan which accentuated his short cropped black hair with tinges of gray. He wore black framed glasses that hung halfway down his nose, as though he was filming me through his diagnostical lenses. On this particular day he was adorned in a powder blue striped seersucker suit, topped off with a printed bow tie. Rather chic, I must say. Truthfully, I wanted to vomit. But compared to my attire-worn out clothes with stains on them-what right did I have to criticize.

"Larry, how was your first night?"

I wonder what your story is? "Fine."

"I understand you're a poet. I'd like to read some of your work. Where can I buy the poems?"

"My poetry is a symbiosis of all that has passed through me, and a continuance of those dead bards whose immortality seeks revenge. Revenge because of America's disdain for artists. I spoke to Walt about this the other day."

"What did he say?"

"Celebrate yourself and sing to yourself, and then the atom shall fall into place. And I do. In the name of the poets I sing to myself and celebrate my time."

"Do you actually hear the voice of Whitman?"

"No. I celebrate life. I have periods where I pick fecundity off the trees. The trees of life."

"You also get depressed?"

"See-saw the clock on the wall it's time to take a fall. Well Doc, am I insane or am I just living in my subconscious?"

"What I think is going on here is that you have periods of mania followed by periods of depression. Furthermore, you have delusional thoughts of grandeur and persecution. Though you may be a talented poet, you haven't been published yet, and you feel the state should support you. You feel all institutions are involved in conspiratorial plots, including this one. This coupled with an obsessive-compulsive neurosis. I'm recommending lithium to control your manic-depressive disorder. The other problems we'll work through in therapy."

I reconstructed only part of the interview. I didn't want to bore you with details about my past, my family, my jobs, and social life. Maybe Doc was right, I'm a depressive maniac. Maybe Doc can cure the world. We should all float in the Dead Sea soaked in lithium. My first impression of Dr. Linton was that he was suffering from a narcissistic personality disorder. He was so self-absorbed, in love with his success and power, and ate it up when I complimented him.

Patricia, a patient on the ward for six months, would sit around all day and knit. This woman could knit until her fingers fell off and then knit some more. On the other hand, Bob would fly paper airplanes all day. Tom smoked all day. And Alan Wainstein would stare all day. He would pick a spot and just stare. Alan very rarely spoke. He's been in and out of mental institutions most of his adult life, suffering with bouts of schizophrenia. To put it bluntly, I was bored. My sessions with Dr. Linton were about the only intellectual conversations I engaged in. Things were kind of copasetic until one day in group therapy I began to liven up the group. Eight of us were sitting in a group led by Dr. Owens, an associate of Dr. Linton, when I stood up and recited a poem:

> Prisoners rapped in gauze
> buried alive
> mummified
> in the House of Bedlam
>
> Dr. Linton waves a wand
> weaving demons
> without reason
> in the House of Bedlam
>
> We do time
> tap on the floor
> walk the hall
> in the House of Bedlam
>
> While the wind blown leaves
> dance beneath the sky
> we chase meds
> in the House of Bedlam
>
> The books are sealed
> beneath coffin planks
> with parasites
> in the House of Bedlam

Searching unknown labyrinths of the mind
empty hands up your spine
dare not question
in the House of Bedlam

The minstrels play
the tunes of treasure
buried in the catacombs
in the House of Bedlam

Chain gangs linked
bust on out
unravel your souls
in the House of Bedlam

At this point my eight comrades began to cheer. I then pulled out from under my chair a bucket of Jell-O, which I stole from the kitchen, and chanted, "The minstrels play in the House of Bedlam." I began throwing the Jell-O, and within seconds everyone was involved in a Jell-O fight. Dr. Owens blew his whistle, and three attendants came to break up the Jell-O fight. I received a stern admonishment from Dr. Linton, with the threat of isolation, if I pulled another stunt like that again. Actually, I thought it was good therapy. The inmates were laughing and having fun. For a brief moment, I restored life where there was death. But I was informed by God there were more constructive means of therapy. There were rules to follow, but rules were anathema to my existence.

That night while laying in bed, I was attacked by Alan Wainstein. I was exhausted and immediately fell into a deep sleep. The attack occurred at 3 A.M. However, I'm not sure how long Alan was in my bedroom. We must have some internal alarm that informs us of imminent danger. Maybe it was the steel gray hollowness of Alan's eyes that pierced into my head. There were no black pupils; everything was gray with red veins as tracks. They stood dangling from an invisible string. I saw nothing but his eyes. I went into those eyes on a journey, a journey that absorbed me, obsessed me, possessed me, and haunted me with a cold grinding of my spine. At 3 A.M., I opened my eyes, and Alan's eyes were hanging above my bed. Steel gray surrounded by a room that was completely black. The optic nerves laser beamed my eyes. I jumped up, frightened of course, and shrieked. My back arched like a feline wanting to claw his eyeballs out of his sockets. "Alan," I yelled.

"You made me laugh."

"Alan, Alan, you can't do this. You scared me to death," as I turned on the light. "It's three o'clock in the morning."

"You made me laugh." That was all Alan could say. I guess that was his way of thanking me. He did promise not to come into my room and scare me anymore. After that episode Alan and I became good friends.

I became quite popular on ward B. I was rather charming at times, other times I was a poet, a comedian, a madman, an intellectual, a confidant. Whatever the situation called for, or whatever whim dawned on me, I transformed into that person. I became friendly with the staff, and sometimes I would hang out in the admissions office. From the information I gathered, the entire staff became frenetic when the minimum number of beds were not filled. Supposedly, this order was a directive from Dr. Linton. They feared Dr. Linton, and did not want to feel his wrath, so they met the quota. The staff acted as though they were giving away free vacations. Meetings were held in regard to how many beds needed to be filled for the monthly quota, and what patient's insurance expired.

Patients were tossed out if they had no means of paying, and often the diagnosis would be falsified to meet insurance requirements.

On a Friday night, Alan pleaded with me to enter Dr. Owens' office. He would not tell me why. He only promised it would be an extraordinary experience. Dr. Owens' office was adjoining Dr. Linton's office. I knew we were breaking and entering, but my curiosity was killing me. Alan was able to jimmy the lock open. The office was dark. I had no idea where I was going, so Alan guided me with his steel gray eyes inside a coat closet. And he was right, it was an extraordinary experience. There were little tiny cracks in the plaster, with tiny beams of light coming through from Dr. Linton's office.

At first I heard voices, and then I pierced through the cracks. I couldn't hear what they were saying, but I saw Janice, the intake worker, sitting on Dr. Linton's desk. He began to kiss her. "Oh my God," I said to Alan, "He's having an affair with Janice." Her blouse became unbuttoned as his hands kneaded her breasts. I was fixated. I was inside a movie. "She's so gorgeous," I whispered to Alan. The skirt came off. She slid down onto him as he sat in his chair. We began to hear grunts and squeaking noises, and then Alan laughed. Dr. Linton quickly pushed Janice off. "Let's get out of here," I said.

We tripped while scampering out of the closet. When we opened the office door, Dr. Linton was standing there bare-footed with his pants on and his shirt unbuttoned. "Welcome gentlemen. Come inside. I want to talk with you." The three of us went back into Dr. Owens' office. Dr. Linton turned on the lights. "What were you doing in here? I heard someone laughing."

"Nothing, we were just acting mischievous," I replied.

"Alan, I'm going to discharge you and send you to a halfway house if you don't tell me."

It was as though a lightning bolt struck Alan's face. He was completely drained of color. "No, no," he yelled. "We were in the closet over there." Dr. Linton walked into the closet. I'm sure he saw the beams of light.

"If any of you tell anybody what happened here today, I'm going to send Alan to a halfway house. Do I make myself clear? Now get out of here."

We left and went back to our rooms. Once again fear dominated Alan's face. "What's the matter with a halfway house?"

"This is my home. I don't want to leave here."

"Alan, this is no home, it's a mental institution. You can make it on your own. I'll come visit you."

"No, no, no," cried Alan. A couple of days after this incident, I was informed that Alan was being discharged. Apparently, Alan was bragging to an inmate about Linton's affair. Dr. Linton discovered the leak, and that was the end of Alan's home in the House of Bedlam.

Two days before Alan was to be transferred, pandemonium broke loose as everyone began yelling and running to the basement. Inside the boiler room, Alan was hanging from sheets attached to a pipe, stone cold dead with his eyes open, staring as if they never left my bedroom. The attendants forced everybody upstairs into the community room where Dr. Owens spoke to us. I was sick. I felt somewhat responsible, but I knew who the real culprit was. I stormed his office in a rage.

"You've got blood seeping out of your conscience. That is if you have one."

"I realize you're upset, but..."

"But nothing, you're a murderer. I know what's going on here. When I first interviewed with Janice, I spoke in my subconscious in lieu of reality so I could enter this place and observe the facility. I never took my meds. I'm a writer and was looking for a story." At this point spit was spraying out of my mouth. "Furthermore, I'm filing a law suit against you for all your fraudulent claims, your phony evaluations for admissions, and for wrongful death. You murderer. I'm going to expose you and your affair, along with the rest of your cult-like disciples." I walked out of the House of Bedlam, never to return.

One month later I was sued by the House of Bedlam for misrepresenting myself. I counter sued for misrepresenting my admissions and intentional infliction of emotional distress. Alan's family sued for wrongful death. Dr. Linton's wife sued for divorce. Janice sued Dr. Linton for palimony. The state sued the House of Bedlam for misuse of funds. There were other suits filed by inmates.

Questions: Was Dr. Linton responsible for Alan's death? By revealing my subconscious did I misrepresent myself or did the House of Bedlam misrepresent my admissions in order to fill their quota of beds?

I read this poem at Alan's funeral:
Entangled with few words spoken
living in a cocoon
Alan created larva with his eyes

Condemned by the judges
without a hearing
Alan refracted light with his eyes

Laughing inside
nothing outside
Alan cried with his eyes

Discerning the truth
meaningless paths
Alan spoke with his eyes

Romance abound
with no feeling
Alan loved with his eyes

Gefilte Fish in the House of Bedlam

A legacy hung
from birth to dust
Alan left me his eyes

Livin' and Lovin' in a Reverie

My love is not reality, but in the mind, a reverie of aesthetics, an eternal bond that satisfies my disconnect with a woman. I've known this for a long time, but haven't expressed it, protecting my ego, enabling me to live in isolation. And then I went to the movies alone, and sat in the last row of the County Theater, with the backs of silhouettes watching *The Visitor*, feeling lonely for the first time ever at a movie. The County Theater in Doylestown, PA reinvented itself several times since 1938. I felt nostalgic walking through the narrow lobby, with the dark hardwood counter displaying confections, and the smell of popcorn popping in the kettle. The seats were stationary, upholstered in the back, with a paisley pattern.

In *The Visitor*, Walter Vale, played by Richard Jenkins, portrays a deadpan robotic college professor who pretends to be connected to his work, but is drowning in a sea of emotionless inertia, disconnected from humanity, void of passion and love.

I sell vintage photos in New York's Chelsea Antique Market for a living, if you can call it that. It's more like survival. My real passion is writing, but after twenty years of six unpublished books, hundreds of short stories, poems, letters, pen pal letters with no replies, a screenplay, movie reviews that I email to people, and a few articles published in newsletters and online, I feel hopeless, calloused, and isolated. I pretend to be happy. I don't want to talk to anybody. I don't want to be friends with anybody, just leave me alone. I think? I'm tired of the deceit, the games, the phoniness. Let me be. And that's the way it's been for the past twenty years or so.

As fate would have it, three immigrants enter Walter's life, and you begin to feel a connection, a birth, an uncovering of the placenta, a symbiosis of what it means to be human. When Walter, who has not been in his Manhattan apartment in years, returns, he discovers Syrian immigrant Tarek (Haaz Sleiman) and his Sensgalese girlfriend Zaniab (Danai Gurira) cohabitating in his apartment. Tarek and Zainab were conned into believing the apartment was unoccupied. Compassionately, or perhaps driven by loneliness and having no passion, Walter convinces Tarek and Zainab to live in his apartment until they can find a place of their own. Tarek plays the African djembe drum in a jazz club and in the streets and parks of New York, while Zainab makes jewelry and sells her wares at a local flea market. Tarek begins teaching Walter how to play the African drum. After playing in Central Park, both Walter and Tarek take a subway to their Greenwich Village apartment. In this era of post 911 immigration crackdowns, Tarek is stopped by a police officer in the subway and asked for identification. The police take Tarek to a detention center and he waits for his deportation as both him and Zainab are illegal immigrants. Tarek's mother, Mouna (Hiam Abbass), arrives from Michigan to lend her support in trying to free her son. Mouna cannot visit Tarek in detention because she too is an illegal immigrant. Walter, who hired an immigration attorney, insists that Mouna stay in his apartment, while the lawyer proceeds with the judicial bureaucracy for Tarek's release.

The doorbell rings. Who could that be, I thought, nobody visits me at this hour.

I open the door to an attractive woman of Middle Eastern decent, olive skinned, jet black shoulder length wavy hair, with dark penetrating eyes, and facial lines that are pathways to a deep life. She puts down her bag, extends her hand and says, "I'm Mouna, Tarek's mom, you must be Larry."

"Yes, yes, yes. A pleasure to meet you, I wasn't expecting you."

"I just got word Tarek's in detention and I caught the last train out of Detroit."

"Please come in, can I get you a cup of coffee or tea?

"Tea would be fine."

"Tarek tells me you hired a lawyer and are trying to help him."

"Yes, I hired one of the top immigration lawyers in NY. But since 911 there is no more leniency, it's cut and dry. If your visa has expired, you're not legal and you are deported. But according to Tarek, he applied for an extended visa after graduating college. The problem is the Immigration Department and Tarek do not have the application."

"I can't visit with Tarek because my visa expired," as a tear rolled down Mouna's cheek.

"I think you should stay here until we get this whole mess resolved."

"No, no, I can't impose, you've been so wonderful to Tarek and Zainab."

"You're not imposing. I insist. You can have Tarek's room. I know this has been traumatic and I feel so bad because I was with Tarek when this happened. I want to help the both of you and make this experience as least painful as possible."

"Thank you. You're very kind."

"Tarek tells me in Syria you were an artist, but stopped painting once you came to the states."

"Yes, I did portraits for the state. My own work I had to keep hidden, it was prohibited."

"What type of painting do you like to create and did you have any influences?"

"I like painting surreal, expressionism, abstract and cubism. The artists who influenced me are Hieronymus Bosch with his allegorical and mystical style, the German expressionists Otto Dix and Max Beckmann, with their exaggerated portraits, of course Dali, Miro, Chagall, Picasso, and the Dadaists with their anti-art. I do collages with my art and I've worked with photos which Tarek informed me you sell."

"Yeah, you'll have to come over to the Chelsea Antique Market and you can look at my photos. I've got thousands of photos and if anything inspires you, take it for your art."

"That's very nice, but I don't paint much of anything anymore since coming to the states six years ago. Tarek's father died when he was six years old, and I promised his dad that I would go to the states with Tarek to see that he got a college education. Sometimes, I've had to work two jobs to help Tarek."

"Yeah, but he's a college graduate now, and you have to get back to your passion. I've been writing for twenty years, and none of my fiction has been published, but I keep writing because it's who I am. It sounds like your art is who you are. I wish I had met you two years ago when Glitter and Doom opened at the Met with Dix, Beckmann, George Grosz and others, exhibiting their work of German portraits. The exhibit left me spellbound. It was as though I was in a night club in Berlin in the 20s surrounded by glitter, billows of smoke, short bouncy bob haircuts, dancing the Shimmy and the Charleston."

There was a brief awkward pause as we stared at each other. I felt happy. I felt connected. We were two artists struggling for recognition with a common goal to free Tarek. But more than that I felt a human connection. I thought about kissing her that first night we met, but I knew it was inappropriate.

"How about you. Who are your influences in writers?"

"Everything influences me; I find motivation in the mundane. As far as writers, I don't read much fiction, it bores me, but Henry Miller and the Beats influenced me early on, probably because they wrote with freedom of form and were autobiographical. Also, I'm very much into Dylan and his lyrical comedic poetry. I am interested in the creative process, in how a story formulates and evolves. Now a days, with the computer and spell check, many original drafts don't exist."

We left the kitchen table at about 5:00 A.M. to our separate bedrooms. I felt certain we could have kept talking indefinitely. I couldn't fall asleep. I layed in bed with my eyes open thinking about Mouna. At 8:30 A.M. my stepfather Bernie called, and woke me out of a sound sleep. "What are you sleeping so late for?" asked Bernie.

"I'm exhausted, I didn't get much sleep last night. Do you have any information?"

"Yes, I spoke to my contact and he's going to see what he can do."

"Whaddaya mean he's going to see what he can do?" I asked excitedly.

"Are you going to start with a million questions?"

"Bern, I'm beggin' you, you gotta help me. Tarek is a good person. He recently graduated and he's never been in trouble with the law. They are going to railroad him out of this country. You know there are no exceptions. He did send in the application for a visa and God knows what happened to it. We were playing the drums in the park and then took a subway, and that's when he got stopped," as my voice cracked with emotion. Bern, you gotta help me, please!"

"I'm doing everything I can. It's going to be alright, stop worryin'."

"Tarek's mom came and she's so wonderful, intelligent, and she's an artist. I gotta help them."

"Is she pretty?"

"Mouna is beautiful."

"Oh, so you're gettin' a little nookie?"

"No, it's not like that, yet. I mean I just met her."

"Don't worry."

"Thanks, I really deeply appreciate this. I can't tell you how much this means to me."

"Ok, I'll talk to you later. But you don't say a thing to anyone about this. You go about your business with the lawyer and let things play out." Every time Bernie says he's going to take care of something it's as good as gold. He works as a civil service employee for the State Department. Bernie is in the business management section dealing with finance. He's been there over thirty years, and knows his way around the White House and Capital Hill. In other words, he's got connections.

When I walked into the kitchen, Mouna was brewing coffee. "Do you have any plans for today?" I asked.

"No."

"Would you like to spend the day going to museums and perhaps catch a play this evening?"

"I would love to." We began our day at the Metropolitan Museum of Art.

"Mouna, do you want see the time line of art? Are you into the antiquities from Egypt, 8000 B.C. to China, 500 A.D., through the 20th century?"

"Yes, I'm very inspired by artists of antiquity and the world through their art, and the fact they worked with hand made tools and developed their own clay and paint. How about you?"

"Wake me up when we get to the 20th century."

"Let's bypass all this stuff," Mouna said.

"No, you've never been to New York, and this is one of the best museums in the world for antiquities. If this makes you happy, I'll be very pleased."

We walked through the time line: the Ming dynasty, the Tang dynasty, the ceramics, the Buddhist stone and bronze sculptures, textiles, woodblock prints, narrative paintings, passing through Tibet and Nepal into the Chinese gallery-it went on and on and on forever it seemed. I became fascinated, not with the art, but Mouna; the way she stopped, walked, and viewed the art, so absorbed, calm, assured, graceful, and beautiful. I couldn't take my eyes off of her.

"Mouna, we've been here about three hours, which is fine and I'll stay, but I wanted to take you to the Museum of Modern Art, and then downtown to the Tenement Museum. Do you want to stay here or go to the MoMA? We can see their modern art collection. But it's up to you. We can always come back to the Met another day."

"No, it's fine, let's go."

We hopped a cab to 53rd Street. Our first stop at MoMA was van Gogh's Starry Night. "This painting has a maddening effect on me. I often come here and sit and stare at this painting for an hour. It's very disturbing and arousing. I feel as though I'm inside the painting and the painting is part of the canvas of New York. And I could die a thousand deaths and it has no bearing. I'm in constant motion with the pulse of the city. I begin to dance and no one notices, because the city is dancing with me. And as I get up from my seat and walk away, I feel like I'm back into my normal routine."

"You're an existentialist," Mouna stated.

"How do you know?"

"I can tell the way you live in the moment, your absurd outlook, and you can't find meaning to your life."

"Is that bad?" as my face turned red with embarrassment.

"No, I find it compelling, and you're very charming on top of it."

Compelling and charming, I thought to myself, as I smiled a sigh of relief. We walked over to Picasso's Weeping Woman and I began another diatribe: "His work aesthetically appeals to me. I think cubism revolutionized art in that it opened up to artists and the world another art form. I wouldn't read into his paintings if I didn't know some of his history with women as a philanderer, many mistresses, an affair with an under age woman, volatile, abusive. He would often leave them poor. Did his volatile abusive ways transfer into his art? Has he stripped women of their humanity, surely their beauty? Has he turned them into raw savages? I see beauty in the art and I also am disturbed because I see pain. Perhaps some of the pain came from the bombing of Guernica. I don't know, but some of his work evokes a wild range of emotions."

"Isn't that the case with most artists, to stimulate your senses," Mouna said.

"Yeah, but we create from our own psyche and his was disturbed."

"What else is new," Mouna decried.

We viewed many other artists, took in some photography, and ate lunch in the cafeteria before heading to the Lower East Side Tenement Museum on Orchard Street. The Tenement is a National Historic site where working class immigrants lived beginning in 1863. The building was left abandoned from 1935 until the museum was founded in 1988. From the outside you walk up about 10 steps with wrought iron railings on each side. Then you walk up three flights of narrow stairs with wooden banisters. You reach the flat, and walk on the uneven wooden plank floors. There are three connecting rooms: the front room, kitchen, and back room with a bed. The total space in the apartment: 325 square feet. The furniture, manufacturing equipment, decorations, and accessories are from the period.

You are living with the ghosts of Harris and Jennie Levine and their five children, circa 1892. Harris and Jennie, who immigrated from Poland, operated a sweat shop in their apartment, working as independent contractors for manufactures of women's clothes. They employed three workers in their apartment: a presser, a baster, and a finisher. Harris operated the sewing machine. Jennie Levine cooked for her family and the workers. The employees worked for the Levine's ten hours a day, six days a week, the legal limit, but probably worked more hours because they were paid four to five cents per piece. The more garments they finished, the higher their earnings. The presser worked in the kitchen, heating twenty pound irons on the stove, and pressing garments on an ironing board. During the busy season, workers often slept in the apartment, as bundles of clothes were used as beds and blankets. They operated their business throughout the year, enduring the stifling summer heat, unimaginable. The bathroom was outside the apartment down the hall. And you had to walk several blocks to the bath house to take a shower. It was unbelievable. We were informed by our tour guide that the Levines were not poor people, but average middle class.

You could barely walk in the back room with its bed and tiny closet. The crib is in the kitchen next to the stove, ironing board, table, and sink. A clothes line hangs above the sink. Above the stove on the wall is a wooden shelf with pots and pans and wooden cooking utensils. On the other side above the table on the wall is a small two door glass wooden cabinet, probably holding dishes and glassware. The front room stored the fabric, the sewing machine, a mannequin, table, chest, and two chairs.

I looked at Mouna, and she too, had the look of awe on her face. I said, "Can you believe this?" She grabbed hold of my hand and we looked at each other for a few seconds, both of us shaking our heads.

I almost forgot about Walter. He's having some trouble. He made a connection with Mouna. They liked each other. And they went out. Walter surprised Mouna with tickets to the Phantom of The Opera. There was one good song: The Music of the Night, other than that I did not like the show. Let Walter take her, I'm not sitting through that boring crap. But the worst of it is-and I feel bad for Walter because I like him-Tarek got deported to Syria. And worse yet, Mouna is going back to Syria to be with Tarek. Walter is devastated.

We get out of the Tenement Museum and Mouna and I are walking on Orchard St. "I have a surprise for you. I have two tickets to the show Blue Man Group. It starts in about an hour. We can grab a quick something to eat or eat after the show."

"I'm alright if you are to eat after the show. What's Blue Man Group?" asked Mouna.

"It's best to see it for yourself, I want it to be a surprise. I've seen it, but I want to see it again with you. It's only about a mile from here."

At the Astor Place Theatre Mouna is looking around at posters of Blue Men wearing blue grease paint on their faces. The show is about a group of Blue Men who never utter a word throughout the show, but instead use mime-like expressions and gestures reacting to a large video screen depicting scenes from our culture, a talkless social satire of performing art and comedy. There is a live band playing music and the Blue Men play music from large PVC pipes. There is also audience participation, and the Blue Men invite someone from the audience on stage to eat Twinkies.

As we walk to our seats we are given two ponchos to wear to protect us when the Blue Men satirize art by splattering paint on paper. During the show, I think Mouna is enjoying it because she is laughing, and she confirms at intermission that indeed she loves the show. When the show is over, rolls of toilet paper are falling from the ceiling and being thrown into the audience from the Blue Men on stage. Mouna and I are literally covered under toilet paper. I looked at her and said, "Isn't this romantic." We both began to laugh and then looked into each others eyes and began making out.

I picked up the toilet paper and said, "This is 1-ply junk, you think they could use 2-ply Charmin for our first kiss?" We went into the lobby and met the members of the cast.

By the time we arrived home at the apartment it was 2:30 A.M., both of us tired, but eagerly anticipating our love making. There was no doubt we were going to sleep together, you could see it in our eyes, feel it in our veins, and hear it in our voices. I played back the answering machine in the kitchen: "Larry, this is Steve Moyer. Little, Brown And Company has accepted your anthology of short stories for publication. Congratulations, call me for the details." Steve Moyer is my literary agent who for the past year was trying to find a publisher for my short stories and novels.

I sit down on the kitchen chair with my head down, my hands covering my face, tears streaming off my cheeks. Mouna walks over, rubs my back and says, "Larry, what's the matter, congratulations, this is fantastic, wonderful news."

"I'm overwhelmed, it's been a twenty year struggle." After washing and brushing our teeth, Mouna and I enter my bedroom, undress and begin making love, passionately, tenderly, talking and looking into each others eyes until 8:00 A.M., when we both fell asleep exhausted.

In the afternoon while having breakfast in the kitchen, I startled Mouna. "I love you."

"We only know each other several days."

"I know. And I'm sorry if I'm coming on too strong. I know it sounds ridiculous, but I know what I feel, and perhaps it's inappropriate to express this now, but I just had to get it off my chest."

"I could see that you always say what you feel."

"Yeah, I know it's a problem sometimes."

"No, I'm flattered, and I've told you these past few days have been the most wonderful for me in a long time."

"I know, we'll give it more time." As the weeks went by, Tarek was released from detention, and was allowed to live in the U.S. while they processed his new visa. Mouna continued to live with me.

On a picture perfect fall day, with the temperature hovering around 70, I decided to rent a BMW M6 convertible, two door in burgundy. I parked in front of the apartment building and called Mouna. "Hi darling, what are you doing today?"

"What did you have in mind?"

"I'm out front. Why don't you come out front and I'll tell you."

"Whose car is this?" asked Mouna.

"I rented it for the day, to take you into the country up in the Catskills."

My dream is to own a convertible. I love driving, especially in the country, with the top down, playing music, free of thought, often in a reverie.

We drive out of the city onto the New York State Thruway, and then onto the back roads. I didn't know where I was at, nor did I care. The air was delicious, Mouna was ravishing, and our hair and spirits were blowin' in the wind as we both sang with Dylan:

How many years can a mountain exist
Before it's washed to the sea?
Yes, 'n' how many years can some people exist
Before they're allowed to be free?
Yes, 'n' how many times can a man turn his head,
Pretending he just doesn't see?
The answer, my friend, is blowin' in the wind,
The answer is blowin' in the wind. (1)

We kept popping in CDs and singing. Both of us couldn't carry a tune. Sometimes we wouldn't listen to the entire song and then pop in another CD until we both liked the tune.

I'm sittin' in the railway station
Got a ticket for my destination
On a tour of one night stands
My suitcase and guitar in hand
And every stop is neatly planned
For a poet and one man band
Homeward Bound. (2)

Oh, the ragman draws circles
Up and down the block.
I'd ask him what the matter was
But I know that he don't talk.
And the ladies treat me kindly
And furnish me with tape.
But deep inside my heart
I know I can't escape.
Oh, Mama, can this really be the end,

To be stuck inside of Mobile
With the Memphis blues again.
Well, Shakespeare, he's in the alley
With his pointed shoes and his bells,
Speaking to some French girl,
Who says she knows me well. (3)

We stopped in the small towns of New Paltz, High Falls, Woodstock, and Rhinebeck, New York, walked and did some antiquing. On the way home I pulled off to the side of the road at this lookout with a mountainous waterfall surrounded by the golden leaves of fall. I kept the car running. "Let's get out of the car," I said, as I played "For Once in My Life" by Tony Bennett. I grabbed hold of Mouna and said, "Dance with me." We began to slow dance.

For once in my life I have someone who needs me
Someone I've needed so long
For once, unafraid, I can go where life leads me
Somehow I know I'll be strong
For once I can touch
what my heart used to dream of
Long before I knew
Someone warm like you
Would make my dream come true (4)

I pull out a piece of paper from my pocket and read a poem to Mouna:

You entered my life as the Weeping Willow
Swept my consciousness through your roots

As I swayed with you in the light
and the ills of plight
Laying with your pendulous softness in the night
The winds of dreams brushed our soul
And the ember stirs, with passions aglow
As this day turns into night, I soundly say
Weeping Willow you mustn't dread
It's loves tenderness I imbed

I hand Mouna the poem, then reached into my pocket, and pulled out an antique diamond ring from the 1920's in platinum with old European-cut diamonds. "I love you. I want to spend the rest of my life with you. Will you marry me?"

I was a little concerned, about the no word, but Mouna jumped into my arms and said, "Yes, I love you." After Mouna called Tarek to inform him about our engagement, we drove off and I played another CD, "Get Me to the Church on Time:"

Jamie, Harry, Friends,
There's just a few more hours
That's all the time you've got
A few more hours
Before they tie the knot, Doolittle
There are drinks and girls all over London,
And I've gotta track 'em down
in just a few more hours!
I'm getting married in the morning!
Ding dong! The bells are gonna chime
Pull out the stopper!
Let's have a whopper!

But get me to the church on time!
I gotta be there in the mornin'
Spruced up and lookin' in me prime
Girls, come and kiss me
Show how you'll miss me
But get me to the church on time! (5)

We drive back to the city and about a half a block from Washington Square Park we hear the beat of drums. I drive by the park where Walter is playing the Djembe African drum. He sounded great as he was bobbing his head to the rhythms, I yelled, "Walter, Walter." He didn't answer, he just kept playing and playing and playing, by himself.

I'm not gonna pretend to be happy anymore. I'm in love and married to a beautiful, intelligent woman. I'm a published author. I've got my own apartment in the Village. I can free illegal immigrants with one phone call. I'm drivin' a BMW convertible. I'm a happening guy. I'm livin' and lovin' in a reverie.

Pick Your Nose in New York

I closed my booth early at the Chelsea Flea Market at 25th and 6th Avenue and headed for the Armory at 67th and Park Avenue to attend a photography show. I waved down a cab outside the flea market, and here's what happened:

After five minutes of riding in the cab, I asked one question. "What's up with New York, why is the traffic so bad?"

"Get out of the cab. I can't concentrate. You're asking too many questions."

Oh my God, I thought, *this cab driver is crazy, what should I do?* "I'm sorry. I want to stay. I won't talk."

Five minutes later I began picking my nose, a nervous habit to release tension, besides my nose was stuffed from the rat droppings and car fumes I breathed in at the flea market, a parking garage during the week. During my first pick the cabby said, "Get out of the cab, you're picking your nose." *Perhaps I should get out of the cab, this guy is a kook, or maybe*

I'm the kook for staying. I'm not going to able to get another cab, traffic is snarled, stick it out, I thought.

"I'm not picking my nose. I was itching my nose. I'm sorry, it won't happen again. I have to get to the Armory." I was scared to do anything. I sat in the back seat with my hands down, not moving my arms or my mouth as the cabby kept a close eye on me out of his rear view mirror.

Thank God we were only two blocks from the Armory when it happened. The cab stopped suddenly in back of a motorcycle, apparently too close for the cyclist. "You motherfucker," said the cyclist, who turned his head and yelled at us in the cab. "Who the hell do you think you are?" The cab driver didn't answer him. Apparently, the cabby only picks on fat out of shape bald men who pick their nose.

When we arrived at the Armory, the cabby flipped down the money draw and I had to force thirteen dollars in the draw in lieu of opening the dividing window. Possibly, he was afraid of germs, I don't know? I walked into the Armory with tension in my veins. *Calm down, you are at the show, just relax, take it easy.* I began to relax as I was caught in a whirlwind of exuberance as each booth was a museum of tantalizing imagery.

Within two hours it was time to leave. I thought it would be best to walk a few blocks away from the Armory, where people were waiting for cabs. It didn't work. After twenty five minutes, I finally got a cab. I almost gave up and began walking back to the flea market, not thinking how exhausted I was from leaving Philadelphia at 2 A.M.

The cab driver was Jamaican, driving fast, with one hand on the wheel, and the other on a hand-held cell phone, weaving and bobbing out of traffic. I was bouncing up and down in the back seat like a bobble-head, and once again I was scared. "Sir, excuse me sir, I don't know if it's safe to drive while talking on the cell phone."

"I do it all the time, mon. I never been in an accident, except some fender benders, mon. Don't worry, mon." *Oh my God*, I thought to myself, *maybe I should get out of the cab.* He was swerving in and out of traffic, making quick, sharp, angled turns, with one hand like he was riding a bronco. And I'm still bouncing up and down in the back seat. He had to be going over the speed limit.

"My name is Larry. I sell photos at the flea market. I just went to the Armory to a photo show. Do you like old photos?" He didn't answer. I thought if I could distract him, maybe he'll get off the phone.

"Watch it, a car cut in front of you," I yelled like I was nervously on speed. He didn't answer.

Maybe I can distract him by picking my nose, thinking he would get angry at me. During my third pick, the cabby looked out of his rear view mirror and smiled, "Pick me a gold one, mon."

The Bizzaro World

I know this has a title that sounds like fiction, but let me assure you this is the truth. All of the facts really happened. Sometimes reality is stranger than fiction. And that's one of the things I love about New York.

I met Wally today at the Stage Deli at 54th & 7th Ave. to buy some photos. We met there last week. I bought some photos. We engaged in conversation, and had a tasty lunch. In other words, it was uneventful. Stage Deli is an establishment that might go back 100 years-check it out on Google. They're notorious for their sandwiches, huge beyond belief, and delicious, especially the corned beef. They are also noted for the plethora of celebrities who patronize the establishment.

To enhance the absurd comedic reality of the story, I am including Wally's hygienic habits. Wally is a nice person and I do feel guilty. I've got no room to talk. I'm no Brad Pitt, and for that matter, no Jackie Gleason on his best day. Both Wally and I have huge guts.

I entered Stage Deli at 11:00 A.M., a half hour before our meeting, and asked for a table. "No," the manager replied, "you must sit at the bar." He didn't want me sitting at a table for half an hour, although the place wasn't crowded.

Apparently, their philosophy is to compress as much humanity into a small space, eating humongous sandwiches while elbowing fellow patrons. Could this be delicatessen bliss, or an indigestible force-fed nightmare? We shall soon see.

I said to the waiter, "I'll take a blintz." Ten minutes go by, and out come three blintzes. One blintz is $5.95, three are $15.95. Apparently, you're supposed to clarify if you want a blintz as an appetizer or as a meal. Excuse me, I thought to myself, I'm from the U.S. and I thought a blintz meant one. OK, no big deal.

In walks Wally. Hygienically, Wally is immature. No, I better say Wally has a problem: Pants: Solid polyester, falling below the waist with boxers showing. Belt: Thick gold buckle worn on the side of his hip, not in the front at his waist.

Reason: Pants too big, and the fly zipper ends up on the side hip. Groovy baby, it's New York. Shirt: Solid polly/cotton-half tucked in, half tucked out. Shoes: Who cares? Sanitation-Clothes dirty. Hygiene: Often needs fumigation, though today, no foul odor.

We sit at a table. Wally orders an open face roast beef sandwich with thick brown gravy dripping out of the plate. An elephant couldn't finish this sandwich. I request a corned beef sandwich. We both ask for water and diet sodas, and I ask for Russian dressing on the side. The food arrives. I ask the waiter if he could please bring our water, and my Russian dressing. Wally begins to eat.

Have you ever witnessed a trash truck grind up its slop, and then the residue leaks out? That's Wally. The brown gravy is dripping around his mouth, and dripping on his shirt. His mouth remains open while he eats.

I had a drop of mustard on my shirt. I stopped and cleaned it with a napkin and water. Yay for Larry. Wally never cleaned his shirt throughout the meal. What is the protocol? This was a business transaction. Wally and I are not social friends. Do you say Wally, you're dripping the brown gravy all over your shirt? Do you slap him in the face with two hands, and say Wally, you need to seek some therapy, you can't act like this in public?

Was I selfish, perhaps worried about insulting him and being unable to buy photos? The waiter passes by and I say, "Excuse me, can I please have some more napkins?"

He mumbles something like Jesus under his breath, and he clearly says, "Are you crazy."

"I beg your pardon," I say. He walks away.

While we are eating, I'm looking at the photos, and the waiter comes back with the napkins and says, "We can't have these photos here."

Response: *Don't piss me off. I'm no animal*, I thought to myself, but I better behave. I've got to buy these photos. "We're in the middle of eating lunch and I have the right to look at photos," I explain to the waiter.

He walks away and mumbles, "You asshole."

I begin to burn like a fire, but still cool as a cucumber. I gotta buy these photos. I can't be distracted. At this point I ask for the manager. Wally is oblivious, he doesn't care what they say or do to me, he's loving that roast beef. I say to the manager, "What's the big deal looking at photos while eating lunch? And your waiter disrespected me."

"We have to turn tables here," says the manager.

"Yeah, well I have to eat without getting angina from management." At this point, the deli is packed, and the patrons take notice as to what is happening. To make matters worse, Wally is towards the end of his sandwich and a big portion of his shirt is drenched in gravy, literally.

Now comes the busboy, a Mexican who takes orders from the Corn Beef Nazi.

He grabs the pickles off the table, and Wally grabs them back. "I got to clear table," he says in broken English.

"This is unbelievable. We are not leaving any tip."

"Oh no, we have to leave a tip," Wally said.

"I'm not." I've got to buy these photos, I thought to myself.

The busboy comes back and grabs Wally's water. Wally yells out, "I want my water."

A few minutes go by, and the busboy grabs something else off the table, it was Wally's plate. At this point I'm fuming, trying to buy photos, eat, and deal with a hostile environment. I stood up and said, "I want to speak with the owner."

Everyone is looking. I shake the owner's hand. "We're getting sabotaged." I begin to get animated, raising my voice, animating gestures with my hands. "My name is Larry Baumhor, and your waiter, manager, and busboy are abusing us. I asked for napkins, and he said are you crazy, and then he called me an asshole. We don't deserve to be treated with disrespect."

"Well, he shouldn't have said that and I'm sorry, but we have to turn tables," said the owner.

"Isn't there any dignity amongst the people who work here?" I asked. I look at Wally, *how about a little support putz,* I thought to myself. But he's finishing his roast beef with a dazed look on his face, not saying a word. He's in a roast beef trance.

I've never been to an establishment with such utter disdain for humanity, I thought to myself. I point to the manager and the waiter. "There they are," I said to the owner.

They come running over, mocking me, saying, "We did it, we did it."

"You don't understand, said the owner, we have to turn tables, you can't stay here."

"We're staying until Wally finishes his meal," I demanded. I'm really pissed, but controlled, I've got photos to buy. Not a word from Wally. "If my name was Larry David in lieu of Larry Baumhor, I bet I could stay."

"Larry David doesn't come in here," the owner responds.

"We'll, I'm gone to Carnegie Deli next time."

"OK," said the owner.

The Bizzaro World

We leave, and it takes me 45 minutes to drive from 53rd to 36th St. at the Lincoln Tunnel. Traffic is gridlocked. I'm driving down 9th Ave, the sirens are ringing in my ear, with police cars and ambulances trying to pass, and police officers running on foot. Probably another shooting. Who cares, I thought. I'm experienced at shootings. I'm weaving and bobbing down side streets like Mohammed Ali, cursing at every manhole and bastard driver in front of me. Finally, I get to the Lincoln Tunnel. It's about 2:30 in the afternoon. I'm stuck at the tunnel for 15 minutes. Some indigent man sitting with the pigeons gives me the finger, except it was his pinky, whatever that means, I thought curiously. I drive by and he yells, "Soul sacrifice."

"Yeah brother," I yell back.

I'm out of the tunnel, unnerved but out of the tunnel. *A valium and a shot of whiskey would work well now,* I thought. Only in New York. No other city in the world offers this madness, culture and art. And for some sick reason, I love it, every minute of it.

I meet a friend for dinner at Michael's Diner at Haldeman and the Blvd. in Philadelphia. We sit in the no smoking section at a table next to the smoking section. While eating my salad, smoke arrives at my non-smoking table. "Ah," I said to my friend in a sarcastic tone, "it's only secondhand smoke."

We are sitting next to a booth that's partitioned by a wall with a circular opening and a ledge. We can see the people sitting next to us in the smoking section. I'm almost finished my dinner, when I look to my left, and see a dog leaning his face on the ledge staring at me. "A lovely dog," I say to the woman. "What type of breed is it?"

"A Toy Fox Terrier," she responds. Am I nuts, but have you ever been in a restaurant where a patron eats with a real dog? Que Sera Sera!

Perhaps it's the Bizzaro World where the opposite is good. Waiters calling us crazy assholes. That's good. Dogs eating with us in restaurants. That's good. Inhaling secondhand smoke in a restaurant while eating in the no smoking section. That's good. Shootouts in the street. That's good. Evil is good. Virtue is bad. Disdain is good. Dignity is bad. I understand this now. If we think all of the bad things are good, which is the opposite of our feelings, then we don't have to worry about bad things. Bad is good. Nasty is nice. Sloppy is neat. And so on and so on. It's the Bizzaro World.

Look at the leader of our country. He invades Iraq to stop nuclear weapons, but the opposite happens. They don't have any nuclear weapons, but Iran does. And he does nothing to Iran. But we're still in Iraq. Osama bin Laden attacks our country, killing our people, and the President does the opposite. He arrests Saddam Huessin, and lets Bin Laden go free. And somehow is able to convince the American people that the opposite, the Bizzaro World is good. It's amazing stuff here folks. Killing is good. Invasions are good. If it's the wrong people and the wrong country, that's still good. And so on and so on. It's the Bizzaro World.

So the next time something bad happens to you, it's really not bad it's good. Just ask our President. He's our leader of the Bizzaro World.

Our Western World

You are cordially invited to a black tie affair, celebrating the year of the sphinx. We shall dine in the womb. Filet mignon, you might ask? Not on your life. Champagne for my guests? Not if I'm the host. The primal flux, the weightlessness, the amniotic fluid where fact and fiction lay fed by a twisted umbilical cord with Eros and Thanatos crisscrossing is where one begins and ends. In the womb reverie prevails, timelessness exists. What happens between the womb of life and death-another revolution, calamity, atrocity, plague?

Unveil yourself. Bring to the surface all that you fear, all that you dare not think of. Come with me you fools, spill your guts and ride with me on the train where we enter gutters filled with filthy rotten lowlife dregs, piss with me in the urinals where a row of phalluses create Davids in all our imaginations, ascend with me where you swirl into laughter always with a slight fear knowing that you too want to escape. You want out.

I swim with sperm through birth canals, weightless, floating like a feather. I swivel my hips in a motion dancing with my lover beating to the pulses, flowing like fire in the wind moving with operatic fluid-eyes on eyes hypnotized by some primitive force spewing out body heat. I am my lover's knight dressed in aphrodisiac words so exquisite that she becomes consumed, intoxicated with romance. I am a beast meandering nude through the jungle, pounding my chest, drenched in beads of perspiration, dancing savagely to the tune of madness. I crave to enter the world of the primordial, to be void of thinking, to run wild like an animal in the jungle.

Change not in the name of progress, but for the sake of freedom. It won't last that long-nothing does, but while you ride your soul shinning through the night shaking the foundation that created you, the ghosts are in flux, you hear melodies you've never experienced, it's phantasmagoria, you have reached your potential-you're floating in the womb of Eros.

The consumer-electric toothbrush. Prestige-the Jaguar. Quick nutrients-the microwave. Unforgettable-CD player. DVD-porn flicks. Ding-dong-the intercom. Ring-the picture phone. Ping-the ice maker. Rrrrrr-the trash compactor. Vibrator-spousal orgasms. Illegal alien-for the kiddies.

I walked the aisles picking up their bones to drink some marrow. I walked slowly through the cerebral cortex with fibers and electrochemical impulses moving like snakes on my body, but never entrapping or strangling me. I walked through the maze of the cortex into the inner wall of the womb and snap the umbilical cord grabbed hold of me. I was drenched in amniotic fluid. I was melting and at the same time regulated by the fluid. I became primitive trying to escape pounding against the womb. I began to grunt. I couldn't think. My breathing was labored. I was inside pounding, beating to a fluid rhythm. Bang-an explosion-amniotic fluid poured out. I relaxed. There was a vision-everything became so clear. The people in the supermarket were looking at me with distorted faces. We fed off of each other- the placenta, the womb, the oxygen, the blood, the nutrients. I could breathe again, and feel blood through my veins.

Look at my life. Look at my success. This is the way to proceed. Bing-the alarm rings-a little shave, a little cologne, a little blush, a dab of rouge, pencil in the eyes, accentuate the lips, scrub the fangs, fumigate the pits and your off. The costume. The masquerade. The power. You need identity. Don't forget the muffin, just enough bran to cleanse the bowels. Beep-beep-beep- fuck you-beep-beep-beep. Now you're revvin' up. Park the car. The smog, the horns, the ants, the metal, the bricks, the doors. The masses. The heads bobbing like wild turkeys waiting to be killed. Puff-puff-puff-a little nicotine. Sip-sip-sip-a little caffeine. Ahh-there goes one heart attack. Burn baby burn-the ulcer attack.

I'm in the valley of the subconscious flowing with swirling ripples of water in a subterranean depth of wholeness where arteries traverse for the poet. Swirl-swirl-swirl against the centrifugal force of my psyche. Chamber wall penetrate me, envelope my consciousness. My neurons fire like diamonds on your surface. I feel my heartbeat with each synch of the sea swells. Each breath I sink deeper and deeper into this dream where the sea is never ending. I ebb and flow with the forces of the tide-a weeping sea urchin silhouetted by my own soliloquy with crystals clanging in my eyes, white caps mystified by the tide. Beat-beat-beat sun of my temple. Your footsteps. Your fervor. As the sky unveils its softness my lifeline passes on. You the sea are my darling, my lover beneath the sky. Everything has turned to steel-the building, your boss, your cubicle. Churn out the paper work, tap the keyboard, pound the hammer. Bing-the register rings. Whistle while you work-slop-slop-slop-slop-slop. Talk-talk-talk-money-money-money. Remember you're steel-nothing can stop you now. Time for lunch. I want to fuck him. I want to fuck her. Don't dare and think like that. The lunch box, the martini, the forced smile, the phony giggle. The bills and more bills and more bills and even more bills. You're trapped. I'm breathing heavy. I'm looking down on myself. I'm a ghost. It's time to go home or am I home. Where am I? I can't see. I can't feel. I can't think. I'm the Money Machine. But look at that greasy guy working the freight elevator and look over there at that pathetic looking cleaning woman and how about the beggar on the street. I'm better off than they are. Right? Well, aren't I? Of course I am. There is no question in my mind who is superior. Rush-rush-rush-rush-rush,...woof- woof-woof-woof- woof...Another day is dawning in our Western world.

    I wandered the streets sniffing like a bloodhound with my back coiled like a cobra always in search of a new form of man. My pads pounding on the hot asphalt. Wrought iron barred windows with minute beds of flowers protruding from the sills trying desperately to exude whatever life a flower petal absorbed. Layer upon layer of brick with black soot oozing from the gutters, the smell of hot lapped tar fuming from the roof tops, the uterus wall shedding its lining clogging the canal ducts, corpus luteum secreting progesterone, while the hot semen soup slides down the epiglottis into the esophagus. The stench of strangled embryos dabbed with perfume clog the drain pipes while bodies sprawl across the top of steam vents. The skulls are bobbing, vertebrates are thumping, ball joints are grasping, cartilage is grinding. The secreting glands are filled with rivers of tales. Always a nightmare. Palates searching for food, the gargling of blood in the throat, the sucking of marrow in the streets, the pounding of metal on metal, brick on brick. The muscles so thick and so atrophied. The perfumed flesh alongside the fouled overcooked crud. Flesh on flesh. The spleen, liver, heart, gallbladder, appendix, pancreas-slopped up on a plate served over and over again. The bile ducts clogged with miniature diamonds cutting into fatty tissue. Arteries and veins tied to the wrong branches. Nerve endings performing like shooting stars bouncing off one another with nowhere to go. Billions of nerve wires malfunctioning, electrocuting. Marrow dripping from the sky drenching the flesh, melting, always melting. The cornea, pupil, iris, lens, and retina dangled on an invisible string while humans walk with their eyes out of their sockets, and their guts sticking out of their stomachs.

In the suburbs success was a substitute for art and culture; everything was shiny and new; prestige and bragging rights were paramount to your soul. Everyone had their own 2 by 4s. Each compartment firing electrical impulses. Appliances, toys, and gadgets fed your ego. Intercoms were strategically placed throughout the palace. The kiddies were forced to perform like pavlovian dogs. While dad was busy at work, mom carpooled the kids from one activity to another, the more the merrier. Sex became an afterthought so one looked elsewhere for relief. You were in a constant vicarious state as boredom began to consume you.

Trapped inside words filled with inertia, the beating of time, the emptiness, the sorrow, the nothingness. Tick-tock, beat-beat goes the clock, swift as the sound barrier, empty as a gun barrel with no bullets, always ticking, always beating. Madness seeping in by the minute, day, year, decade until the stench of death has dried up your senses like a prune that's been dried not by the sun but by the beating of time, like a woodpecker pecking on a bark except the bark is your skull.

I sit and wait for what I don't know because nothing matters and yet everything matters. I bathe in the soap of inertia laying in my tub lathered with bubbles that take up space. Which one will burst in the air? Which bubble will reach the ceiling? Why be a slave to the master of time? I think I'll go for a walk on Hollywood Boulevard searching for a reflection in the windows of fame.

Are you armed? Are you fed up? Are your nerves frazzled? Do you take a hit of Xanax in the morning? Are you running to mother's little helper? Have you reaped what you sowed? Flip flop the burger goes on the grill. Sss-sss-sss. Pop. Crackle. Sizzle. Frazzle.

Another year. But it's Labor Day. A day of fun in the sun. Farewell laborers, farewell. Happy trails are here until we meet again.

I waited in line under the El where we all looked like a bunch of rags waiting in line for some cleaning fluid. Pathetic faces, souls without hope. As the train rattled on the track, the corroded pillars peeling with rust began to shake, cars double parked puffed with steam venting from their overheated engines, taxis huckstering and the local whores proselytizing while I waited and waited. Now the vibrations began to get hold of me. I was aboard the train riding to nowhere, traversing the valleys, the hills, the nightmarish cities. Yes, I was on the dream train. Nothing but destiny at my doorstep, and the faces of Americans staring through the window waiting in line, always waiting. Their wrinkled crevices, slanted eyes, worn out skin, with their hearts over their shoulder in a knapsack just like the hobos. The line of a thousand faces, of a million faces, of a trillion faces. Starving babies screeching in my ears, helpless with nowhere to go, always on the train, always in line, always waiting for something. On the train and in the line everybody is waiting. In the factories, in the offices, on the construction site, everybody is waiting, everybody is riding the train. It's the vibration of life. It's the train and destiny of no-mans land. All aboard. Choo-choo-choo. All aboard. Choo-choo-choo. All aboard. Choo-choo-choo. Our Western world!

Poems for Strippers

    I had to improvise, I had no money, I was horny, on welfare, and suffering through yet another 100 rejections as a writer. For 20 stinkin' dollars my friend Michael literally hounded me to death to be his designated driver. He already had one DUI in New Jersey. Destination: Playland, a strip club on route 120 in Barton, New Jersey, a town suffering from postmortem manufacturing. It looked like Desolation Road with empty factories, winos, harlots, pimps, and drug dealers occupying the town. In 1994 I was 41 years old, only five years of accumulating unpublished manuscripts.
    I owned a 1980 Ford Fairmount, a beige four-door station wagon. The bastard was approaching 200,000 miles, leaked oil like a drippy faucet, and sounded like a Harley-Davidson. Twenty bucks was a lot of money to me in 1994. I had no job, well, to be honest, I couldn't hold a job. I can't tolerate authority, I prefer poverty and independence. If some smart ass boss got uppity with me, I'd tell him to go fuck himself and

walk off the job, right in the middle of the day. I even threw my ex-wife out of our apartment after an argument. Her father called me a bum and I told him too to go fuck himself. Probably, I had some kind of mental condition or something.

The only income I had was the $190.00 I received every month from welfare. I'd go to flea markets and sell old books, ephemera and photos, but couldn't seem to make any money at that either. Welfare also gave me food stamps. Every week I'd take the food stamps to about ten different Wawa's and 7-Eleven's and buy one banana. I'd pay with a one dollar food stamp and get about eighty cents change, depending on how big the banana was. I accumulated about nine bucks, enough for a movie, a box of Goobers, and a couple dollars worth of gas. Gas was only $1.15 a gallon.

I never went to a strip club before. I was embarrassed, thought it was perverted, and had no desire, but 20 bucks was 20 bucks. I was offered a job, and informed by Michael it would be on a regular basis. I was a strip club driver. We entered Playland, immediately sat down at the bar, and began watching the girls dance.

"I'm buying you one coke, you have to sip it the whole night," Michael said.

One stripper leaned over the bar and placed her tits near Michael's face. My heart started to pound. Michael placed a dollar in her cleavage. And then she placed her tits near my face. "I'm sorry, I don't have any money. I'm a starving artist, an unpublished writer." *What a putz, I don't believe you just said that. Like a little 41 year old baby, you don't have any money, you're a starving artist-na-na-na-na-na, stick your head in gravy, baby.*

Oh shit, I thought to myself, what the hell was I going to do for two hours? Perhaps I'll wait in the car. "I'm going to wait in the car," I informed Michael.

I go in the car and am flushed. I'm all worked up and I got a little erection on top of it. There's got to be a way to breakdown the money barrier. Poems, I'll write poems. *You'll write poems, you big putz. Who do you think you're dealing with Emily Dickinsons? These are frickin' strippers for Christ's sake. They pretend to like you and take your money to the bank.* You don't think they have feelings? *Feelings for cash. Get a grip. Save the idealism for your writings.*

I went back into the club and sat next to Michael. I asked the bartender for a pen. I took hold of a napkin and began to write. The first poem I gave to a stripper, who smiled and walked away. *I told you putz.*

I began composing another poem on a napkin. I was into this now. People were beginning to talk. I heard whispers of, "That guy is writing poems on napkins and handing them to the girls."

Your smile, your cheer
Represents no fear
Your heart, your eyes
Seek no lies
If only I knew
More of the lore
Your words become true
Demystifying morning dew
"What's your name, baby," Nikki asked?

"Larry. I'm sorry I can't give you any money. I drove my friend Michael, because he drinks. And I'm an unemployed writer tying to get published."

"You don't need money," as Nikki placed my two hands on her breasts. "This is the sweetest thing anybody gave me. You're my Baby Poet," as she kissed me on the lips and walked over to the next patron.

I'm her Baby Poet. I felt like crying. I felt spacey and warm, all fuzzy inside. I made a connection. She took my breath away. Long brown, flat, thin hair with full sensual lips, high cheek bones, and dark penetrating eyes, the eyes of my muse. Her body was tight, but not muscular, and her stomach was flat, her waist cut with natural firm breasts that accentuated her aura. If only I could be with her, I daydreamed. My muse, my wife, the mother of my child. I could write into the wee hours of the morning. *Listen to me you loser, you haven't been laid in 4 years and that pecker of yours is fuckin' with your mind.* Yeah, like she's not diggin' the poetry?

Nikki comes out from behind the bar and sits down next to me. "What type of stuff do you write," she asked?

"I write novels, short stories, poems, essays, and I like letters, but no one answers me. I write what I like to call self-confessional fiction, stream of consciousness. I hate the literati, plots, structure and detailed descriptions. It bores me. I was influenced by Henry Miller, the Beats, and Dylan."

"I'm takin' a poetry class at Temple, and we're reading Ginsberg. Howl is pretty wild shit."

"Howl is my favorite poem. I met Ginsberg at Penn, and after his speech, he autographed Howl and Kaddish. Like a schmuck, I sold the books at a flea market for ten dollars each. I was talking to him about genre literature. And he said keep writing and be true to yourself. Do you have any major at Temple?"

"I'm majoring in psychology. But I'm not sure. My dancing pays for college. I love to write too, but there is no money in it."

"I'd love to read your writing."

"Ok, I'll bring a copy of my short story for you to read." Nikki got up, it was time for her to dance again. Oh my God, she loves to write, she likes Ginsberg. She wants me to read her story. I love her, I thought to myself. *You love her? She's twenty years your junior. You're a fat bald man on welfare with no prospects, a wannabe writer with five years of unpublished manuscripts who can't hold down a job.* Hey, screw you, I know a connection when I see it.

I began writing feverishly on a napkin. Poetry was dripping from my lips. I was surrounded by magic, her name was Nikki. I was in a whirlwind. Nothing mattered. I was going to ask her for her home phone number. I was going to ask her out, a relationship, and then marriage, everything would be ideal.

Mystery eyes
Weeping eyes
Tender eyes
Ghosts in your eyes
Past lovers in your eyes
Entrapped in your eyes
Rebirth in your eyes

Nikki finished dancing her two songs and walked over to me. The bar was filled with patrons. Why else would she come over to me if she didn't like me. I handed her the poem. She straddles her legs around my waist, hugs me, and then places her two hands on my cheeks, stares me in the eyes and says, "You need a couch dance, don't you Baby Poet?"

"I don't have any money."

"Your poems and your soul are money. Come with me." She grabbed hold of my hand and walked me into the backroom. I was about to get a free couch dance. It was a small dark room with three small sofas and music speakers. A burly weightlifter type of guy stood at the podium near the entrance counting the girls' dances, and I guess to keep order. Boy, was this degrading, I thought. Here I am sitting in the middle of a couch with another guy sitting at the opposite end and a stripper groping him.

Nikki was topless wearing only a G-string. She sat right on top of me-wasting no time- as I began to knead her breasts and rub her stomach. "How's my Baby Poet feel, nice, hot, and hard?"

"Yes," I responded in a breathless tone. Nikki began licking the inside of my ear. And then she began giving me baby pecks on the lips with her lips. "Nikki, thank you," I moaned, as I began to hold her waist, lifting her in motion up and down, lost in her eyes, I exploded. In less then two minutes I was done. I couldn't make it through one song.

"Let me go wash up, I'm wet," Nikki said. I was embarrassed, realizing my pants were wet and so was her bare skinned leg.

"I apologize. This is embarrassing."

"No problem, my Baby Poet, this happens, it's part of the business," as she grabbed hold of my hand to lift me, we then walked out into the main room holding hands. I love her even more. *You love her even more. You really handled Nikki well. Cut me a break. She's patronizing you, she finds you amusing like a circus freak.*

Nikki let go of my hand near the end of the bar at the entrance to the back room where all the strippers changed. As she opened the door, she said in a loud tone, "I've got a comer on me." The girls laughed.

Children of Baseball

When in need of Little League coaches, who do you call? Jocks. Who else but those tobacco-chewing, gob-spitting, biceps-bulging, bull-charging, in your face jocks. I was one of eight coaches from my son Andrew's Little League team. We were supposed to teach seven and eight year old kids baseball, sportsmanship, and camaraderie, and in the process have a lot of fun. But it didn't turn out like that. We weren't real coaches and we weren't jocks, but we thought we were. We had beer bellies, lived vicariously through our children, ranting and raving on the ball field like wild dogs frothing from the mouth, playing Lombardi type baseball. Who cared if we didn't set an example for our kids? This was 1990s baseball and we were real men who chewed tobacco, ate quiche, and pussy. We all lived in the suburbs.

Our lovely suburbs with our lovely half acre, with our lovely plumbing, with our lovely neighbors, with our lovely children. The barnyard pets with their fleas and ticks howled. Hot asphalt streets were being rolled. The shrubs sprouted their little buds. Everything was new and clean. There was even a delightful metallic smell to the sewage pipes, unclogged as the garbage was dumped pell-mell. Yes, all the drains were in top order. Consumer appliances were in abundance: electric toothbrush, microwave, CD, VCR, intercom, picture phone, ice maker, trash compactor, and a vibrator, all mandatory in the suburbs, so cunning, forlorn, and filled with prestige like the Jaguar sitting in the driveway. Spousal swapping and cheating was a rite of passage as most waited for the kids to leave for college before they left their spouse. Boredom, school board meetings, kid's activities, and testosterone poker games filled your days. The more after school activities for little Johnny and Stephanie, the happier mom and dad were. The children were tested for special academic classes giving bragging rights to the parents. Carpools and bright yellow school buses dropped the kiddies off at local suburbia institutions for a day of brainwashing.

As for our children, they were imbued with life's innocence, gaiety, and soon to be burdened with shaping our destiny into the twenty first century. But for now they were angelic creatures of our planet. I saw that twinkle in their eyes-you know, the one that says, I can reach for a star and ride it through the night. They knew nothing about winning and losing and grinding your opponent to smithereens. They weren't corroded with corruption and obsessed with money-earning money, spending money, transforming into money, never enough money, always craving more money. They didn't have to worry about the rent or food or being squashed by another human in the war of climbing corporate America. Our children weren't concerned about economics, racism, and American capitalism. They were just free spirits hoping to catch and hit a little ball with a little metal bat and tag some bases. It all seemed so innocent-baseball-America's favorite pastime.

During our first practice, little Bobby, with his bifocal glasses falling off his nose, was unable to hit the ball, not so much because he couldn't see, but because no one could throw the ball over the plate-he was that small. And then there was Jimmy-he was the tallest-a natural athlete, but he was gawky, and when he swung the bat, he swung up and down and everywhere but where the ball was. And then there was Crystal-a spunky little girl who ran the bases even though she never hit the ball.

Andrew, my son, smashed the ball every time at bat and scooped up everything in the field. No doubt about it, he was the best player on the team. And no doubt about it, I wanted him to get a hit every time at bat, though I never told him that. It was always, "Don't worry Andrew, no one hits every time at bat, we're out for fun, to meet new people and to learn, it doesn't matter if you strike out." And that's what I told the kids-it's ok to strike out, it's ok to make an error, as long as you're having fun and you keep trying. I would give all the kids high fives and words of encouragement, even when they struck out. "Good swing Bobby, good hustle Jimmy."

That's the way it's supposed to be, fun, camaraderie, and learn a little baseball. But that wasn't the feeling I had in my gut. There was something deeply rooted in the core of my being that no matter how hard I tried to dig out the rotted roots of winning, competing, crushing, and being the best you could be, the roots enveloped me, swallowed me, ate at my synapses-there was no way to escape it and I was petrified. These were my kids-innocent little children playing an innocent little game, many of whom were participating for the first time. I had to make this a rewarding experience. I owed it to my kids. I owed it to my own flesh and blood. But I was dealing with a cancerous war, one so ingrained in the American fabric that even I, the love child of the sixties, the pacifist of the ninety's, the seeker of benevolence, the beacon of souls, could not unravel the cancerous root of war-kill or be killed.

What do you expect? Look around you. Everybody wants to crush you. Grind your opponent into the ground. The cost we pay for this destructive competition is death. The death of not only the human body, but the death of your living soul. We're at war on a daily basis. Look at the battles you go through at work everyday. The constant driving to be number one. Be the best you can be. Don't even ask questions, just send the boys home in body bags. Kill off cultures and races of people. Commit genocide. Go ahead. Play your war games. Knock him out. Build your weaponry and destroy. You're number one. America is number one. Ahh-the burning of ash-it feels so good. Push harder. Drive further. You're almost there. Push a little further. A little harder. Come on you can do it. Number two isn't good enough. You're almost there.

After our first practice, I received a phone call from the commissioner requesting that I attend a meeting. The commissioner was an ex-jock turned slick lawyer who thought he was father of the year. The commissioner summoned the meeting as a result of the other coaches complaining that the teams were unbalanced.

"We're going to have to restructure this league, because some teams have too many eight year olds and others don't," the commissioner stated.

"I want to keep my same kids. I don't care how old they are. I like my kids."

"Larry, you can't, because your chances of winning will be diminished because you have mostly seven year olds," said the commissioner.

"You're going to have an angry bunch of parents. Every parent wants their kid to stay on my team."

"Alright, you can keep your kids."

During our first game my kids had to hit the ball from a pitching machine. The kids had never before practiced with this ominous creature, and they all struck out with the exception of Andrew who had one double. The league didn't allow the teams to practice with the pitching machine. I felt bad for my kids. Here they were during their first game, being mowed down by a machine releasing a ball at fifty miles an hour, ossified with fear, smoked out by a gun, a shootout at the O.K. Corral. One by one they fell, dejectedly their spirits sank.

Our children stand at the plate holding a bat, a glove, a racquet like brave little soldiers; just like the children in Iraq, they ask no questions and have no complaints. And we the parents, not President Bush, have no answers. Like the President, I kept cheering them on with a false sense of hope-come on Jimmy, good hustle Bobby, you'll get'em next time Crystal.

The bottom of the second-I'll never forget this-our team was on defense and the bases were loaded. A ground ball went through little Johnny's legs who was playing shortstop, and landed at the feet of little Jimmy, who was playing left field-actually right behind shortstop. The only thing Jimmy had to do was pick up the ball and throw it towards the pitcher, which would have stopped the play. Jimmy picked the ball up and cocked it in his hand and then froze. Our bench was on the left side of the infield and I began to yell, "Jimmy throw the ball to the pitcher." And then I began to yell louder, "Jimmy throw the ball to the pitcher." And then I began to scream, "Jimmy throw the ball to the pitcher." But Jimmy stood frozen, unable to move as all four runners circled the bases. The grenade was there, he just couldn't pull the pin. "Don't worry about it Jimmy-nice play Jimmy," I said, as he ran to the bench.

The opposing team was bigger and stronger, and the coach was hungry for blood. The coach yelled at his kids for missing the ball, and would pull them out during the middle of an inning. One poor kid began to cry as the coach hounded him for poor defensive play. "How many times have I told you to get in front of the ball, let it hit you in the chest, don't be afraid of the damn ball. What's the matter, does your leg still hurt?" asked the coach. The kid slid into second and hurt his leg the previous inning.

The kid answered, "Yes." But I knew it was the kid's pride that was hurt, not his leg. He was crushed by a warmonger. I felt like spitting in the coach's face. Instead, we all shook hands at the end of the game. We lost 18 to 0.

During the playoff game my assistant coach Steve almost got the shit kicked out of him by the opposing coach. Steve, who was coaching third, informed his son Seth while running towards third to knock down the third baseman and run home. Fortunately, there was no contact, but the opposing coach stormed the field and got right into Steve's face. "Are you fuckin' crazy, telling your kid to knock down Tim. I oughta knock the shit out of you!"

There was a big brew-ha-ha at third base. I finally calmed Melvin down. "Mel, he knows nothing about baseball. I apologize. It shouldn't have happened. I'll have a talk with him." The truth of the matter was that Steve really knew nothing about baseball. I guess he knew nothing about common sense either.

To make matters worse, I got thrown out of the game for arguing balls and strikes. I was a schmuck. And then at the end of the game Steve, my assistant, informed me that Mel didn't call some of his kids who were not good ball players. Supposedly, a parent informed Steve. Like an idiot and sore loser, I got into an argument with Mel. "I was informed you didn't call all your kids."

"That's a lie. I called all my kids. I can't help it if some don't show up."

"That's not what I heard, maybe I should protest this game," I said. I look back on this and think what a putz I was. I had no evidence that this occurred.

The season ended and the kids became acclimated to hitting off the pitching machine. We even won two games. Andrew made the all star game. Of course he was chosen, he batted 18 for 28 during the regular season and had some dazzling plays in the field. I kept stats, not unlike the casualties during war, everything was measured in numbers, body bag counts, and money spent by the Industrial Military Complex. Andrew was the clean-up hitter during the all star game, the big RBI man. I took my camcorder-just in case he made it to the big leagues, I'd have something for those sound bytes. First at bat-Andrew struck out. Second at bat-Andrew struck out. He always made contact. It was incredible what was going on. "Maybe it's the pitching machine," I said. "Don't swing at every pitch and step into the ball, you're bailing out of the plate."

Third at bat-Andrew struck out. "Don't worry about it, you're doing well. I'm proud of you. You can't get a hit every time. You made some great plays in the field. You had a tremendous season. You have a lot to be proud of. I love you. If it wasn't for you the team wouldn't have won those two games. It's only a game. Sometimes the big league players feel bad." But Andrew was worried, he fought back the tears as one rolled down his cheek. I thought maybe it was the pressure of the big game and the fact many of his relatives were there.

The game was tied in the last inning when Andrew's team was on the field. I heard somebody in the stands say, "I hope he doesn't get a hit. Maybe he'll think about getting hit by a car." I moaned nervously, however, I should have suckered the guy.

Andrew batted in the bottom half of the last inning; his team was down by two runs, and the bases were loaded with two outs. All season long he was the Ted Williams, the Ty Cobb of baseball-even better than they were. He delivered game in and game out. "Ball one," called the umpire. Foul tip. "Ball two." My body tensed up-I couldn't watch, but I forced myself. My little boy of seven-the hero-the villain. If God was watching, I wanted him to come down and let me take Andrew's place-let me bare the pain. I prayed-if not God send me some angels.

But it was not to be, no God, no angels, not even his dad could help him. He was all alone, although his buddy's were loaded up on the bases. He stood bravely at the plate with just a metal bat. Swing and a miss. "Strike two," shouted the umpire.

A cowardly voice screamed out from the stands, "Strike out the bum."

Remember, he's just a little boy, for it's moments like this we should open our hearts. So please don't forget, they're only little children and not men and women yet.

Gefilte Fish

Have you ever eaten smoked gefilte fish, not with the traditional horseradish, but with a couple of cigarette ashes on top, billows of cigarette smoke in the air, served by a Jewish Grandmother who wore a brassiere as a blouse, with a Viceroy cigarette dangling from her lips? My Grandmother, who I called Nanny-don't ask me why, no one knows-would carry a tray around the room, and take a piece of gefilte fish on the spoon and flop it onto your plate. "Here doll, here's another piece of fish," plop. She would never take the fish and gently lay it on the plate. Sometimes, it would flop down from as high as two feet in the air. On several occasions she missed the plate.

My Grandfather, who I called Zayda, would chain smoke Viceroy cigarettes and drink schnapps out of a shot glass. "*L'chayim*," (To life!) he would say in a thick Romanian accent, and down went the schnapps. Now it's time for a Viceroy cigarette. Zayda would attempt to blow the smoke up to the ceiling, but it permeated the room. After the cigarette, "*l'chayim*," he would say again, and down went another schnapps. Then another cigarette. Then another schnapps. This continued throughout the evening. He was addicted to nicotine and alcohol. I never smoked a cigarette in my life, thanks to Zayda. Steve McQueen thought otherwise as he advertised on television, "When I'm off stage I smoke Viceroy. A thinking man's filter with a smoking man's taste, Viceroy."

Zayda, whose Jewish name was Hain Benikes, was born in Beltz Romania, 1908. At the age of 12, on December 31, 1920, Zayda and his mother, my great-grandmother, Sarah Benikes, arrived at Ellis Island on the passenger ship Caronia. I researched this information on the Ellis Island web site at www.ellisisland.org/, and amazingly discovered all of these details, including a passenger record, a photo of the ship, and a Ship Manifest that stated: "States Immigration Officer at Port of Arrival. States, or a port of another insular possession, in whatsoever class they travel, must be fully listed and the master or commanding officer of each vessel carrying such passengers must upon arrival deliver lists thereof to the immigration officer. Steerage Passengers Only. Arriving At Port of (stamped) New York (stamped) 31 Dec 1920."

Many of my Zayda's relatives, such as brothers, cousins, uncles, brother and sister-in-laws were listed on the Ship Manifest. Many questions were asked on this manifest, like whether you're in possession of $50.00 and if less, how much? Have you ever been in the United States before? Are you joining a relative or friend, and the name and address of such a person?

The condition of coming to the U.S.; your health, mental and physical, height, color of hair and eyes, marks of identification, and place of birth.

Zayda and my great-grandmother Sarah immediately moved to Philadelphia, Pennsylvania's Marshall Street, where relatives helped them settle. They changed their name to Samuel and Sarah Berman. I could not find any information on Zayda's father. Marshall Street was a bustling community of Jewish immigrants, yapping away in Yiddish, who were alive with a cultural vibe of religious freedom, and the dream of prospering while earning a living.

Thank goodness Zayda left Romania in 1920, as the anti-Semitic propaganda and violence against Jews heightened throughout the 1920s and 1930s by the Iron Guard, culminating during the Holocaust in the murder and death mostly by Romanian authorities of 280,000 to 380,000 Romanian and Ukrainian Jews. Besides Germany, Romania killed more Jews than any other country.

Marshall Street was the hub for shopping in Philadelphia, with merchants operating retail stores, and hucksters selling their wares from pushcarts set up at the curb. Zayda and Sarah operated a pushcart, selling schmaltz herring and pickles. It must have been quite a scene with the two hucksters selling their schmaltz herring and pickles to the bargain hunters who wanted better prices. Zayda never attended school in the United States, as he had to help Sarah with their pushcart business.

Nanny came to the United States when she was a child from Russia. Not much is known or can be researched about her, except that she too had no education, and married Zayda when she was sixteen years old. Nanny's maiden name was Mildred Cohen, and she gave birth to my mom, Barbara, at the tender age of sixteen. Barbara gave birth to me at the age of twenty. How did these children raise children? Nanny and Zayda, two hot-blooded, uneducated European Jews, fell in love on Marshall Street amongst the schmaltz herring and the Yiddish yapping, and created a family.

Passover is a celebration commemorating the exodus of the Jews who were freed from slavery in Egypt. The Haggadah, read at Passover, is a book about the Exodus and the rituals surrounding the Passover Seder. Some of the rituals are blessings, pouring of the wine, with questions like: ("Why does this night differ from all other nights?") asked by the youngest child. The meal includes unleavened bread and bitter herbs. The Jewish people were told to make meals in haste, thus there would be no time for leavened bread. The herbs symbolize the bitterness of slavery.

At Nanny and Zayda's Passover Seders there was no reading from the Haggadah, no unleavened bread or herbs, no reading of the questions, no blessings, no rituals, nothing to indicate we were attending a Passover Seder, except maybe the gefilte fish. Nanny even served bread and butter. I didn't even know the Jews were enslaved until my mid twenties when I started college. How could I? I didn't attend Hebrew school. My mother hired a shyster rabbi who only taught me my Bar Mitzvah part.

Gefilte Fish in the House of Bedlam

The family would meet at my grandparent's apartment the first two days of every Passover. The dining room was so small that when the extra leaf was attached to the table you had to turn sideways to pass at the backend of the table, if not you would hit the wall. The kitchen, where Nanny performed her culinary art, was about 7 by 10. Eight family members attended the Passover dinner: My mother and brother Fred, Uncle Moish, (my mother's brother), and his two kids, Susan and Glen. Fred and Susan are five years younger than I, and Glen is ten years younger. And let's not forget the host and hostess, Nanny and Zayda. My father abandoned us when I was five years old. Uncle Moish's wife left him after five years of marriage.

In the spring of 1973, I was twenty years old when the family met for Passover dinner. I brought my best friend, Gary Mills, who was attending his first Passover dinner as a gentile. The only shock for me was seeing Uncle Moish transformed into Mickey, the groovy, free-spirited, gold-chain-wearing hipster. He had a thick afro hairdo, with a thick mustache and long bushy sideburns. He was wearing a black and yellow geometric pattern Nik-Nik shirt that was so tight it looked like the nylon was going to burst off his body. The first three buttons were open with a gold chain around his neck. He had on orange polyester bell-bottoms and black boots with high heals.

"Uncle Moish," I said shockingly.

"I'm Mickey, call me Mickey, can you dig?"

"What happened to you?"

"I'm just groovin', man."

That's a sin, I thought to myself. Uncle Moish was thirty six years old in 1973. I hadn't seen him since the 1972 Passover dinner. Uncle Moish always had a crew cut, no mustache or sideburns, and dressed conservatively. He's about five foot six with striking features. He joined the Navy out of high school, and would always come visit me when I was a kid. He'd scare me half to death with his antics, like putting his two thumbs together back to back, and tucking them under his curled fingers, pulling the two thumbs apart as though they were becoming detached. I would scream and run upstairs. I was sad. I loved Uncle Moish. I didn't like Mickey.

"Uncle Moish, I mean Mickey, this is my friend Gary."

"Cool, man cool."

"Nanny and Zayda, this is my friend Gary."

"How do you do," Zayda said in his Romanian accent.

"You seem shy. *A goyishe kop*, (slow-wittedness) but a *haimish ponem*," (friendly face) Nanny said.

"Nan, are you startin', I said.

"*Feh*, (an expression of disgust) *vus* (what) I do now?"

"Mom, the soup is cold," Barbara, my mother said.

"*Kvetch*," (complain) Nanny said, as she reached over my shoulder, grabbed my spoon, and tasted the matzo ball soup. "*Oy vey*, (exasperation) you *schlemiel*, (a habitual bungler) Sam."

"I heat soup, *vus* you want from my life," screamed Zayda in his heavy Romanian accent.

"Heat the soup, it's ice cold. Did you heat it under ice cubes?" screamed Nanny. Nanny and Zayda constantly screamed and fought over nothing. You could not be with them for more than an hour without them screaming at each other. I only wish I had a camera, because I could have been a wealthy documentarian.

'Tis soup warm," shouted Zayda.

"*Meshugeneh*," (crazy person) yelled Nanny, "Get out of the kitchen."

After the soup, Nanny came over and dropped matzo balls on your dinner plate. Matzo balls were heavy and laid in your stomach. They are made from matzo meal, eggs, water, schmaltz, and baking powder.

"Here's a ball for my Larreleh," Nanny said. She always called me Larreleh, never Larry, and she always referred to a matzo ball as a ball.

"Nan, please, I can't eat it, I had two in the soup."

"Mildred," screamed Zayda, "he doesn't want matzo ball."

"*Mitten derinnen*, (all of a sudden) you're the maven," hollered Nanny.

"*Sha*," (Shut up!) shouted Zayda as he lifted his arm up in the air and threw it down in a motion of disgust, and then picked up his shot glass and downed another schnapps.

Now it was time for Nanny's ritual song and dance that I named The Larreleh. You never knew when she was going to perform this song and dance, during or after the meal. She went into the adjoining living room and began singing, wearing a white brassiere with her cleavage showing, an apron wrapped around her waist, and a pair of slacks, dancing barefooted. "My Larreleh, my *tatteleh,* (endearing child) I love you, ta, ta, ta. My Larreleh, my *tatteleh,* I love you, ta, ta, ta." And then she started clapping and singing as she walked over to my friend Gary, clapping her hands near his face. "My Larreleh, my *tatteleh,* I love you, ta, ta, ta," Gary began to clap; he didn't know what else to do.

The next portion of the meal Nanny served was the gefilte fish. Every time you finished one gefilte fish another was thrown onto your plate. "Nan, that's enough with the gefilte fish," I said.

"*A bissel,* (a little) *ess gezunterhait,*" (eat in good health) Nanny replied.

"Mildred, *genug iz genug!*" (enough is enough) screamed Zayda.

"Nanny, can you please stop smoking the cigarette when you're serving?" I asked. "You just got an ash on Gary's plate."

"Oh, the *k'nacker,* (big shot) is telling me how to serve."

"Let me serve," stated Zayda.

"Sit down, Sam," demanded Nanny.

"Give me the plate," Zayda yelled.

"Get out of here," screamed Nanny.

Uncle Moish put his head down and began to cry hysterically. "I can't take this anymore," cried Uncle Moish. My mother got up from the table and walked over to Uncle Moish and began rubbing his back, "It's alright Mick, it's ok." I later discovered that Uncle Moish had a cocaine problem. He eventually enrolled in the 12 step addiction program, became a counselor, and shed his Mickey image. Mickey left and Uncle Moish returned.

Nanny continued to serve, dressed in her brassiere, with a cigarette in her mouth as she brought out the sweet and sour meatballs, brisket, chicken, *varnishkes,* (kasha with noodles) and roasted potatoes, placing all of the dishes on the table. Thank God she didn't serve them individually. In all the years of Passover dinners, I never once saw a vegetable on the table. You became bloated like a stuffed carbohydrate.

After dinner, I invited Gary into the bathroom for the carp ritual. I opened the bathroom door, and swimming around in the tub was a twenty pound carp. Nanny believed that you could only make fresh gefilte fish the day before you served it. So on the first night of Passover, Nanny made gefilte fish for the second night of Passover dinner. I often remember going to the Jewish deli with Nanny and Zayda. I would carry the metal basin into the deli. In a gigantic wooden vat carp were swimming around. The deli man always told Nanny that the carp were freshly caught. He would then fill up our basin with water and a carp. We would drive home in their 1969 Buick Four-Door Sedan. I sat in the back seat with the carp while my grandparents argued in the front seat.

At the edge of the tub Zayda got down on his knees holding a wooden mallet in his right hand, and as the water drained from the tub the carp began gasping for air, flopping around in the tub. "Bang, bang," Zayda tried to hit the carp, but missed. We were standing at the entrance to the bathroom as I looked over at Gary, he was mesmerized.

"Hit it in the *keppele*, (little head) hit in the *keppele*," Nanny yelled.

"*Shvayg!*" (Shut up!) screamed Zayda, as he killed the carp with one firm knock on the head. Zayda took the carp into the kitchen, where Nanny cut the head off the carp and deboned it. She then took out of the refrigerator a few fresh white fillets of haddock, chopped up some onion, a carrot, and mixed in an egg, salt, freshly ground black pepper, and a couple of tablespoons of matzo meal. She would knead the ingredients together with her hands and briefly place the ingredients into a blender. She then wet her hands and shaped the ingredients into diameter balls, placing them on top of onion leafs in a glass baking dish filled with a drop of water, and then baked the gefilte fish.

Within five years of the 1973 Passover dinner Zayda was diagnosed with cancer of the larynx. A surgeon removed his voice box. He died within a year, still screaming all the way to his casket. Also, within five years of the 1973 Passover dinner, Nanny ended up in a mental institution. I often visited her, and in the lounge area with other patients she would sing and dance: "Larreleh, *tatteleh*, I love you, ta, ta, ta."

On one occasion, I began singing and dancing with Nanny, "Larreleh, *tatteleh*, I love you, ta, ta, ta," as the other patients joined in and began to clap. Nanny died in a nursing home of Alzheimer's. The nurse informed me that hours before Nanny's death while lying in bed in a barely audible voice she was singing, "Larreleh, *tatteleh,* I love you, ta, ta, ta." I kind of miss those days.

Driving home with my friend Gary from the 1973 Passover dinner he said, "This was fantastic, what an incredible tradition."

"Unfortunately, this is not tradition," I said, "this is a dysfunctional family."

In 1975, at the age of 22, I ended up on a psychiatrist's couch. I remember sitting in his waiting room when Dr. Kozman entered and asked me to fill out a brief questionnaire. I answered the usual questions about health, insurance, family history, and then it asked: Give a brief description of why you are seeking therapy. My two word response: Gefilte Fish.

Your Disco Buddy

In 1977, at the age of 24, I was a disco dancer. I assumed everyone in their 20s in 1977 was a disco dancer. That was the year of Saturday Night Fever, mini skirts, maxi skirts, bell-bottoms, Lycra stretch pants, Nik-Nik shirts, halter jumpsuits, satin jackets, platform soled shoes, afro hairdos, people doin' their own thing, not carin' about me and you.

When the weekends hit, you went to your local disco and boogied to the likes of: Don't Leave Me This Way (Thelma Houston), I Will Survive (Gloria Gaynor), Disco Duck (Rick Dees), I Love The Nightlife (Alicia Bridges), Disco Inferno (The Tramps), You Sexy Thing (Hot Chocolate), I Love Music (O'Jays), Shake Your Booty (K.C. and the Sunshine Band), and Stayin' Alive (Bee Gees).

In Philadelphia, the hot local disco was Second Story at 12th and Walnut St. The club was on the second floor of a former five story Episcopalian School and Church. The disco was in the chapel with a twenty foot high ceiling. The music from the sound system reverberated off the walls, penetrating you, forcing you to feel good about yourself and dance the night away. The lighting system, with neon and mirror balls that rotated around the ceiling, transformed you into a John Travolta fantasy. There were several small connecting rooms off of the dance floor, where I remember making out with chicks.

Not unlike the famed Studio 54 in New York, you had to be accepted at the door. You had to either look like a disco duck or have a membership card. I don't remember why I was fortunate enough to have a membership card, but I did, and that's the gist of this story, a membership card to the legendary Second Story. I recently found this membership card while rummaging through some old boxes. The card is a testament to how cool I was, and how good looking I must have been to get a membership to Second Story, at least I had a full head of hair and was thin.

Every Friday night for 52 weeks in 1977, I went to Second Story with my friend Debbie Meyers. Debbie was friendly with my girlfriend at the time, who was away at college. Debbie and I had a strictly platonic relationship, though I must say she was quite a catch at 5 foot 8, blonde, blue-eyed, a soft spoken affable person with an infectious smile, and not a deceitful bone in her entire body. After 1977, I lost contact with Debbie, never to see or speak to her again, until I found my Second Story membership card. As soon as I found my membership card, I thought of Debbie. Our relationship is bound by a disco club.

There has to be some way to contact Debbie, I thought. I located a person who had Debbie's email.

After thirty years of not talking with Debbie, I decided it wasn't good enough to just contact her and say I found my membership card to Second Story. I wanted to blow her away with an exaggerated prank, an Andy Kaufman routine. Andy, one of my favorite comedians, though you dare not say that around Andy, who thought of himself as a "song and dance man." I created this story of how Second Story was reopening and invited Debbie to the gala opening. Here is the email I sent to Debbie, none of which is true except that I did find my Second Story membership card.

Hi Debbie:

How are you? I hope things are going well. Did you get an invitation to the reopening of Second Story? I received an invitation in the mail for the last weekend in June. And get this: I have a free one year membership, available to anyone who produces their old Second Story membership card. Perhaps you have yours laying around in a box somewhere, or maybe it's mixed in with your doll collection or any other collectibles you might have saved as a kid. If you open up the attachment, you'll be able to see my membership card. I was thinking maybe it will bring back some memories of where you placed your membership card.

The new Second Story is located on Sansom Street around the corner from the old location at 12th and Walnut. They're having a big gala opening celebration. For the opening weekend, you have to dress in 1970's attire. I couldn't find much I saved from the 70s except a lot of photos. I looked pretty good back in the day. My hair stopped growing and most of it on top is gone, so if I go to the opening, I'll probably buy a wig and some bell-bottoms. I found hidden in the back of my closet, a shriveled up Nik-Nik shirt, a mid-night blue geometrical pattern. If you remember, Nik-Nik used a tight qiana fabric that clung to your body. Unfortunately, I remember washing this Nik-Nik and it shrunk. I can't even get my arm into the shirt. I always dry cleaned my Nik-Niks.

The new Second Story is going to have three dance rooms: disco, ballroom, and freelance. I haven't danced at a club in a long time, but about a year ago I got inspired by Dancing with the Stars, and took a few ballroom dance lessons. It didn't go well. It was a group class. During the Cha cha my instructor became upset with me and said, "Larry, 1, 2, Cha-cha-cha, this is not a disco class, 1, 2, Cha-cha-cha." Members of the class began to laugh. Ah, *kuck im on* (the hell with them) to the Samba Kings and Queens of Northeast Philadelphia, who were very serious and intense about dancing.

And then for the Foxtrot, I felt like a donkey hewhawing across the dance floor. Afterwards, my partner, who looked like a Lisa Rinna wannabee with collagen lips and augmented breasts, stared me down with a stern admonishment, "You're not taking this seriously."

"I am, I just can't do these dances."

"Didn't you dance as a kid?" she asked.

"Yeah, I won a pimple ball at a twist contest when I was about 12, and during the 70s I would disco."

"Sure," she answered sarcastically.

"Did you ever hear of Second Story?"

"No."

"Well, Second Story was the Studio 54 of Philadelphia, and I had a membership."

"Oh," she replied.

I left ballroom dancing behind, and took a pottery class. That didn't go too well either. You had to mix and make your own clay. I never got the thing right: The clay was either too soft and fell apart or too hard and wouldn't mold. I had to use my classmate's clay, or my teacher would make extra clay for me. I was like a mad scientist, mixing copper oxide, ball clay, borax, sand, and glaze clay. I quit the class. Another klutzy attempt at culture and art.

At any rate, sorry about the digressions. Let me know if you're interested in going to the opening of Second Story, and if you can locate your membership card. I think I can get Steve in too.

Your disco buddy, Larry.

Here's Debbie's email response:

Hi Larry:

Wow! Talk about a blast from the past. I don't even remember having a membership. At least you're still dancing. I don't dance anymore. I'm sorry, I can't go to the opening to Second Story. I have graduations, Bar Mitzvahs, and a wedding the entire month of June. Let me know about the opening. And stay out of those back rooms. What have you been doing for the past 30 years?

Your disco buddy, Debbie.

That's a good question, what have I been doing for the past 30 years?

So Your Kid Wants to be a Sportscaster

So your kid wants to be a sportscaster? Talent alone may not be good enough. The availability of jobs is far less than the demand. This, of course, creates an imbalance, forcing the future voices of tomorrow to live in no-man's land, an obscure market covering local sports for pennies on the dollar, living off nickels and dimes, scraping, scratching, clawing, hoping, dreaming their break is just around the corner. I'm talking about veterans. If you're a rookie like Andrew, just out of college, where do you begin? How do you even get in front of a mike when the sportscasters with experience are scooping up entry level jobs?

Andrew's dream evolved in my apartment at the age of eleven, when innocently enough, while watching the Phillies game, I said, "Andrew why don't you turn the sound off and broadcast into the boom box?" Andrew took the mike, and began to record his first broadcast. Literally, my jaw dropped as I became startled, almost frightened by his innate ability to describe the game, poised, descriptive, and exciting. A star was born. Andrew, I said, "That was amazing. I'm in shock. You should do this for your career. You're really good." The seed was planted. Wait, here's what else I said to him. "You're as good as some professional broadcasters."

"You're crazy dad."

"I'm serious, you really are," I responded.

Andrew was on board with the idea of becoming a sportscaster since inauguration day in my apartment. For crying out loud, what kid that likes sports would not want to become a sportscaster, especially if their father keeps telling the kid how great he is and that he or she-let's be politically correct-should be a sportscaster when they grow up.

On May 13, 2007, Andrew graduated from American University majoring in Broadcast Journalism. Andrew was a star in the sports broadcasting community at American University. Andrew was funny, irreverent, informative, and he would ad-lib analogies during play-by-play broadcasts, as a panelist on SportsZone,-a talk show, and as a sports anchor on college TV news. When I started watching and listening to the DVDs and CDs Andrew would send home from college, I thought the good Lord sent me a combination of Howard Cosell and Bob Costas. Hallelujah! Drewy is going to ESPN, screw those smaller markets, I dreamt. I got a genius on my hands. I was handing out DVDs and CDs to anyone and everyone, like a huckstering whore gone mad.

Andrew made a contact with Marc Zumoff, the Emmy award winning sportscaster for the Philadelphia 76ers. Marc is the founder and president of Your Airtime at www.marczumoff.com. Marc offers a comprehensive range of services for News and Sports Anhors/Reporters, and Play-by-Play Announcers. He was very gracious with his time in giving advice and critiquing Andrew's performance after watching and listening to his tapes. Here are some of Marc's comments via email: "You're knowledgeable. You're funny! Your content is good and one key here-you looked right into the camera and ad-libbed. That's a great quality. Not many (highly-paid even) people in our business can do that and be comfortable with it. You did put on some exciting stuff first-that's a good thing. It's probably one of the top 2-3 things people look for in announcers. Your court description is good. You've gone to great pains to package yourself (DVD, CD, folder, plastic) and that's a good thing. Anything you can do to make yourself stand out is good. You seem to have many of the right tools (energy, enthusiasm, talent) and I think you will ultimately be successful in this daunting but not impossible task." Well, that's all I had to hear from nine-time Emmy Award winner Marc Zumoff. Now I was getting cocky, why not dream for the stars, I had the kid going into the Hall of Fame. What's the difference, he'll skip a few steps.

I spoke with Andrew about applying for jobs early and began sending his resume package to employers before graduation. With graduation in May of 2007, we began the process of mailing resume packages to employers on October 18, 2006, seven months before graduation, and if you were lucky, you didn't have to be an employer to receive the Holy Grail.

The resume package is sleek and sexy and pops out at you, a professional masterpiece that father Picasso designed. Three different color laminated folders were available.

Inside the folder, on the left and right side, are pockets for Andrew's resume, cover letter, CDs, and DVDs. On the left pocket, there is a slot for Andrew's business card. Folder number 1 was black. "Come on down," as the announcer for the The Price Is Right would say. Folder number 2 was gray. And folder number 3 was blue. The reason for the different color folders was that if an upgraded resume package was mailed to the same employer, there would be a color distinction. Andrew's resume was placed in an 8 ½ by 11 clear plastic top loader, archival, mind you. At memorabilia shows, dealers display photos or collectible paper inside the plastic top loader. The resume and cover letter are printed on 32 pound 100% cotton paper. You had to order this paper from a cotton/pulp farm down south. This was a very delicate process, as I had to be sure the future Hall of Fame broadcaster was represented with an aesthetic presentation that matched his genius. The plastic top loader with the resume was placed inside the right pocket, and the cover letter was placed on top of the resume. Two business cards were developed by my friend Steve, a graphic designer, and one was placed in the left slot/pocket. One card, purple and black, designed with a photo of Andrew broadcasting with head phones, was used for radio sports talk and play-by-play. The other business card was blue and yellow with a silver mike popping up on the right side, used for anchor/reporter positions. I had jewel case size photos of Andrew, either as a sports anchor in a suit and tie, or broadcasting play-by-play. I used Andrew's photo on the outside of the jewel case, and Andrew's CD or DVD demos were placed inside. Gold color DVDs were used for his TV demo, and silver color CDs were used for his radio demo. The CD and/or the DVD was placed inside the folder on the left side, and on top of the cover letter in the right pocket.

Andrew applied for play-by-play, radio, and TV positions, including anchoring/reporting, sports talk, and various combinations of radio jobs that included sports broadcasting, airshifts, sales, and news.

We both knew Andrew would start his career in a small market. We kept upgrading his demos. We had the ammunition. With Andrew still in school, seven months away from graduation, Operation Andrew was in full swing. I researched jobs, burned CDs and DVDs on my computer, created the resume package, and mailed it to employers.

412 and 85, 10-18-06, 8-03-07, 0. Do these numbers mean anything to you? They do to me. 412 is the amount of resume packages Andrew and I mailed to employers. 85 is the number of new upgraded resume packages mailed to employers who received the old resume package. 10-18-06 is the date we began to mail resume packages. 8-03-07 is the date I'm writing this, and the last resume package I mailed until tomorrow. 0 is the number of full-time job offers Andrew received. In a nine month period we mailed 412 resume packages and 85 upgraded resume packages, totaling 497.

Can't get a full-time job. No job. It appears the number one sportscaster in the world, the genius Hall of Famer, is unemployed before he becomes employed. As I write this with tongue and cheek, a feeling of sadness swarms over me, a depression, frustration, anger, questions answered and unanswered, guilt feelings, and then there is a revival. You are knocked down, bloodied and battered with your front teeth knocked out; you get up and spit your bloody teeth in your opponents face. The opponents are the employers. You need this metaphorical attitude, otherwise you are defeated. Defeat will not happen. Andrew has too much talent and passion. And for me, I'm just a dad trying to help his son fulfill a dream, as I wipe away a tear from my face.

I began to feel a heavy burden gnawing at my existence. As the conductor, perhaps I orchestrated Andrew into a never ending composition, an on going saga of small town markets with department store like pay. Suppose he could never make a living at this, I thought? What guarantees are there in life?

"I was sitting at my new desk at my new job- weekend sports anchor/reporter at WPBN-TV in Traverse City, Michigan. It took me about ten months to finally land this position, but a few days into it, I was already having my doubts. Traverse City, known for its brutal winters, was under 2 feet of snow. I didn't know the town, I didn't know the people, and I didn't know how I could live on 16 thousand dollars a year- before taxes," Chuck Garfien said in his article written on ComcastSportsNet.com. Chuck is a reporter/anchor for Comcast SportsNet Chicago, and a former anchor for ESPN and ESPN News.

Upon graduation, Andrew received his diploma, and a bill for $65,000.00. That's how much debt he was in. In college, I would tell Andrew, "You're like a doctor or lawyer learning their trade. You'll pay it back in no time." What a crock of shit!

If you met Andrew, the furthest thing from your mind would be that he's a broadcaster. He's quiet and reserve. Even his vocabulary is different on the air, as he pulls out words that he never uses in real life. Perhaps he is Tony Clifton the lounge singer, alter ego of Andy Kaufman, Andrew's favorite comedian, though you dared not say that around Andy, who thought of himself as a "song and dance man." Andy was probably more of a performance artist, like Andrew. And perhaps Andrew Baumhor is the ultimate lounge singer when he performs with his mike; he seems to be role playing like Tony Clifton. Andrew does Kaufmanesque things, like flying to Boston to visit a friend in his dorm in the middle of the night unannounced. While in Australia, Andrew thought of a plan to have a fake doctor come visit him at his house and have the doctor claim he was dying, but decided against that prank, thank God.

After mailing 412 resume packages, Andrew received four interviews. A simple question has to be answered: Why could Andrew not get a full-time job during a nine month period of mailing 412 resume packages, 85 upgraded resume packages, totaling 497? "And finally, you will need to have patience and extremely thick skin. Expect to be turned down for literally hundreds of jobs in your career. If you are not, that only means you didn't send out enough resume tapes," stated Chuck Garfien from Comcast SportsNet.

There is no short answer nor is there one answer, a multitude of answers are the reason for Andrew not getting a full-time job offer. I'll list ten answers in no particular order and then elaborate: 1. Your first job after graduating college is the most difficult to land. 2. Young college graduates enter a job market with more qualified experienced applicants than there are jobs available. 3. We sent out some resume packages where there were no jobs available and to jobs that required broadcasting experience other than college. 4. Andrew needed improvement on some of the beginning broadcast demos. 5. American University does not know their ass from a hole in the ground when it comes to helping sportscasters obtain jobs. Poor quality broadcast equipment was used and a poorly structured resume was recommended. 6. Some jobs are posted in order to satisfy EEO requirements when the employer already knows who they are going to hire. 7. Andrew looks too young. 8. Andrew does not know how to interview and blew job opportunities with Kaufmanesque responses. 9. Andrew is passive and would have conflicts with his father in regards to not following up after the initial resume package was mailed and upgrading his TV demo. 10. The old adage of it's not what you know but who you know that counts.

Your first job after college is the most difficult to land: "You are both to be commended for your persistence. Unquestionably, the first job in broadcasting is always the most difficult one to get," Jon Chelesnik said. Jon, the president of www.staatalent.com, has years of professional broadcasting experience, including the host at ESPN Radio Network, and is dedicated to helping both novice sportscasters like Andrew and seasoned professionals.

"These are tough times for sportscaster-types. From the down-sizing of sports networks, (such as Fox Sports Net), to the total elimination of others, (such as CNN/S), to the reduction, and, in more and more cases, elimination, of sports departments at local television affiliates, opportunities for sportscasters are vanishing at an alarming rate. The end result has left the sportscasting industry more cut-throat than ever, so much so, I know many experienced and talented folks who are either out of work or getting out of the industry all together. The road to sportscasting success will be long and hard, if not impossible," Dave Benz said, the CEO of www.sportscastingjobs.com.

I often have therapy sessions with my sportscaster psychiatrist Dr. David Brody, who informed me that not only is the first sportscasting job difficult to obtain, but sportscasters with years of experience have trouble securing jobs. As a novice sportscaster, Dr. Brody sent out 100 tapes when he lived in New Jersey without receiving a response, until one year later WIP, a sports talk show in Philadelphia contacted him. David Brody, president of Broadcaster Marketing Services at www.sportscastingcoach.com, is a three time New Jersey Radio Sportscaster of the year winner and was a sports talk show host on Sportsbyline USA from 1993-2003. Dr. Brody offers a full line of services to both rookie sportscasters and veterans. He represents sportscasters, helps in the preparation of

TV and radio demos, books sports guests for both TV and radio, and coaches sportscasters, his beloved passion. He offers psychiatric help as well, especially to neurotic fathers who have all but gone mad from the overwhelming task of helping their child become a sportscaster. Dr. Brody has spent hours of psychiatric sessions on the phone with me without charging a fee. I think Dr. Brody does pro bono work for severe cases of sportscasting disorders. Thank God for psychiatrists!

The old days where each individual college hires their own sportscasters is coming to an end, as corporations are selling broadcast packages to many colleges and conferences, offering them a wide variety of products, including broadcasters, radio and TV coverage, promotions, web site management, marketing, advertising, event management and promotions, corporate and client entertainment packages, customer hospitality services, signage sales, licensing, public relations, and more. These companies will sell you the kitchen sink, but the key is that they supply colleges with sportscasters. We mailed 7 resume packages with no shot at landing any job to ISP Sports, Nelligan Sports Marketing, Big Ten Network, Learfield Sports, and Host Communications. If a broadcast position opened at any of these companies, they will do the hiring, not the college. You could be the best play-by-play sportscaster in the world, but it appears they operate like every other business, and often these corporations hire from within.

I would make calls to the networks and affiliates to try and get the appropriate contact to mail a resume package. This in itself was maddening, because I sent resume packages to a person who didn't do the hiring, only later to discover that another person did the hiring. I solved that problem by asking to speak to the president of the company. The big shot Dad from Philadelphia wants to speak to the President of CBS. He's got a resume package of his son who hasn't even graduated college with an over-modulated tape that must be delivered to the appropriate person who does the hiring. What a putz! Don't laugh, it worked. I often spoke with the secretary of the president and was very honest, stating, "My son, Andrew Baumhor, is a sportscaster and he's in his senior year at American University, and I'm trying to do research to find out who the person is that hires the sportscasters." I would engage in several minutes of conversation with the President's secretary and she would give me the appropriate contact of the person who does the hiring. Sometimes the secretaries would make comments like, "Oh, it's so nice to help your son." They should only know what I was going through. I was doing extensive research, burning CDs and DVDs, mailing out hundreds of resume packages, while inundated with paper work and broadcast material all over the apartment. Not to mention, being under the care of sportscaster psychiatrist. And I've got a kid who won't follow-up, and thinks he's Andy Kaufman during an interview. Wonderful!

We mailed out 24 resume packages to personal contacts. In other words, if you once shook Chief Halftown's hand, you were a contact. If your uncle's friends aunt's brother lives next to Ed Snider's first wife's cousin, you were a contact. If your neighbor is the assistant manager of the maintenance department at the Wachovia Center in Philadelphia, you were a contact. All kidding aside, most of the contacts weren't long shots, but none made a bit of difference.

I had the balls to send 9 resume packages to agents while Andrew was still in college. I had Andrew so wacked out that he informed me if a good offer came in, he would consider leaving college and finishing later. "You're not leaving college early," I said, as though there was a possibility he could get an offer.

Andrew needed improvement on some of his beginning broadcast demos. The most important benefit of sending out resume packages seven months before Andrew graduated was that we learned what areas needed improvement, and then made the appropriate corrections. From October 2006 thru July 2007, a ten month period, we continually upgraded the demos. Some of the upgrades were minor, just removing one track, and in some cases a new demo was needed.

In January of 2007, with only four months left in his college career, we began to send out resume packages to TV stations in smaller markets throughout the country. We sent a resume package that included two DVD's of both SportsZone and anchoring/reporting. "A program director will not play both tapes. You need to combine Andrew's SportsZone with his anchoring/reporting and create one tape," Dr. Brody stated. Dr. Brody helped Andrew create a new anchoring/reporting tape from the material we sent him.

Dr. Brody stated that the length of Andrew's DVD demo was inappropriate. "Program directors do not want to look at long tapes, and Andrew's is too long," Dr. Brody said.

I began resisting therapy. "While Freud at first saw resistance as an obstacle to uncovering the unconscious, he later recognized it as something not simply to be overcome, but as an important element in psychotherapy. The origin or source of these resistances were, and are still, seen by many therapists as residing in the client. The therapist bears little, if any, responsibility for client or patient resistance. Resistance is a defense; defense is a response to a threat. Therapist interventions can be, and often are, threatening to the client. Interpretations are often threatening to the client," C. H. Patterson stated from the article Resistance In Psychotherapy: A Person Centered View. After all, he's my son, not Dr. Brody's.

After five months of no job responses, I realized Dr. Brody was right, and we did another TV demo eliminating the extended anchoring and the play-by-play. Although we still would send out the extended anchoring with the play-by-play TV demo for radio job play-by-play positions, along with Andrew's radio demo. I know all of this sounds confusing, like Abbott & Costello's Who's on First. But believe me, I was going crazy and would try anything. Nothing seemed to make a world of difference as we hit 412 resume packages with no full-time job offers. Still anguished over the rejections, frustrated with the task at hand, saddened by depression, and in pain as I felt Andrew's struggle in the pursuit of a job, we marched on, the three of us, Andrew, myself, and Dr. Brody down the path to sportscasting nirvana.

In the fall of 2006, Andrew's senior year, I suggested to Andrew to contact his career counselor, and find out how to proceed in the job market. Andrew and I had not met Dr. Brody at this time, nor did we engage in any job research. Andrew met with the career counselor, and asked how he should proceed to get a job as a play-by-play announcer. "I don't know any jobs available as a play-by-play announcer. No one has ever asked me before. You better look into working at another job," the career counselor said. There you have it. The dream was over. It didn't start yet and it's over baby. Over my dead body! I thought this was amazing. Did this idiot ever hear of the Internet? Does she know how to type in sportscasting jobs on Google where you would find www.sportscastingjobs.com, www.staatalent.com, www.sportscastingcoach.com, and other sites that have hundreds of job listings for play-by-play announcers? Does this counselor know all the accolades Andrew received as a sportscaster? Has this person ever listened to Andrew broadcast a game at American? I was infuriated, and told Andrew that this was an example of the first obstacle you'll overcome. This was the moment that I informed Andrew not to worry, that I would help him pursue his career as a sportscaster. Operation Andrew officially began as a result of an incompetent career counselor at American. With Andrew's talent and my tenacity and perseverance in untangling bureaucratic systems, I felt I could somehow will Andrew to success. I felt a special power. How dare this career counselor try and crush Andrew's dream before it began. I felt invigorated, strong, nothing was going to stop me. I didn't care what sacrifices I had to make. I felt empowered.

Mister Trouble never hangs around
When he hears this Mighty sound:
Here I come to save the day!
That means that Mighty Mouse is on the way! (1)

Under my direction, I was like General Patton, storming ESPN with a barrage of nine resume packages from 10-25-06 thru 3-12-07, including five to ESPN TV, three to ESPN Radio, both in Bristol Connecticut and one to ABC in New York. Two of the nine resume packages were sent to the Human Resource Departments at ABC in New York, and ESPN in Bristol Connecticut. For some reason, I wasn't cognizant of the fact that ABC, Disney, and ESPN are one Company. The problem is when you call ESPN, they will not tell you who does the hiring. I had to research, dig, probe, and read. I kept getting different names. I should have just went up to Bristol, Connecticut, and stood in the parking lot and handed out resume packages.

Nine months later on 7-16-07, Mickey, a real image of him on the letterhead, responded to Andrew by mailing back a beat up and tattered resume package along with the following letter:

Dear Mr. Baumhor:

"Your recent submission was received by one of our Company's business units. However, while we appreciate your writing to us, our Company's policy prevents consideration of your submission. As a matter of long-standing policy, the Walt Disney Company does not accept unsolicited creative submissions. Please understand that the policy's purpose is to prevent any confusion over the ownership of ideas that the Company is working on or considering. Compliance with this policy on unsolicited submissions is the Legal Department's responsibility, and that is why your submission was given to us for response. We are returning it to you without having reviewed it or retaining any copies of it in our files.

Thank you very much for your interest in the Walt Disney Company."

Even Mickey Mouse rejected us!

If a broadcast company wants to hire specific play-by-play, sports talk, and anchor/reporter broadcasters outside their company, they are prohibited by EEO requirements unless they advertise for these positions. To advertise and interview other candidates for a position that is already filled is circumventing the law. And herein lies the dilemma. I'm sitting at home like Mr. Putz sending out over 400 resume packages and some of the positions are not really available. It's all make believe. It's a fairy tale.

> *Tale as old as time*
> *True as it can be*
> *Barely even friends*
> *Than somebody bends*
> *Unexpectedly*
> *Just a little change*
> *Small, to say the least*
> *Both a little scared*

Neither one prepared
Beauty and the Beast (2)

Andrew looks too young: First it was Dr. Brody informing me Andrew looks young and might have a tough time landing a job in television. Dr. Brody and his staff stated that Andrew's hair needed to be cut, and that when he makes a TV demo he could use some make-up. This doctor is as crazy as a cuckoo bird, I thought. Andrew created his TV anchor/reporter demos while a senior at American University. Some of their equipment is cheap, often broken. He had no headset, let alone a make-up department. "Suffice it to say, with all due respect, college kids sitting around in jeans will not cut it for a demo reel. If you can, put on a jacket and tie and style your hair (of course, I'm jealous since I have none!)," Marc Zumoff stated in an email to Andrew, regarding his SportsZone TV show.

On June 19, 2007, I mailed a resume package to Darren Haynes, Sports Director at WBKB-TV in Alpena, Michigan, a CBS affiliate. The job was for a weekend sports anchor/reporter. You also had to shoot during the week. You needed 0 to 2 years experience. On 6-29-07, Andrew spoke to Darren Haynes, who said Andrew was a top five finalist for the job. He watched Andrew's TV demo and said, "You have a lot of creativity and energy. But you look too young. It's a disadvantage. You have a baby face."

Baby Face,
You've got the cutest little baby face.

There's not another who can take your place,
Baby Face.
My poor heart is thumpin',
You sure have started somethin',
Baby Face.
I'm up in heaven when I'm in your fond embrace.
I didn't need a shove
'cause I just fell in love
with your pretty baby face! (3)

Darren Haynes informed Andrew not to worry, that he once didn't get a job in TV because he looked too young, and suggested Andrew take a radio job for the time being.

"Andrew," I said, "that's positive feedback, and you were a finalist for a TV job."

"How is it positive, I can't get a job for ten years?"

I'm sending out 400 resume packages, no one is helping me, I ain't got a pot to piss in, and now I got a kid with a baby face who can't get a job!

Andrew did not know how to interview and blew job opportunities with Kaufmanesque responses: On June 21, 2007, a resume package was sent to WPBN/WTOM-TV in Traverse City, Michigan to News Director, Doug DeYoung. The job was listed as a sports outdoors/reporter. "Successful candidate will be someone who can dig up local stories each day." On July 23, 2007, Mr. DeYoung called Andrew for a pre-phone interview and stated that, "You are in the final top 5 out of 40 tapes." I mean this was incredible, now we are getting somewhere, I thought.

During the interview, Mr. DeYoung asked Andrew, "Why do you want to become a sportscaster? What are your goals? What are your challenges?" This was a three part question and needed an expanded response.

"I want to broadcast TV in a top 10 market and do play-by-play for a pro team," Andrew responded. That was the extent of Andrew's response. He said nothing else. Suffice to say, Andrew never heard from Mr. DeYoung again.

"You're kidding me, right?" I said to Andrew when I heard this.

"That was my answer."

"Are you Andy Kaufmann or Andrew Baumhor? I'm confused. I need a serious answer. Because I don't know who you are. We've had discussions on how to respond to these types of questions. Andy Kaufmann would deliberately sabotage his comedy routines and purposely do bad performances to upset the audience. I'm sitting home sending out these resume packages. Now I need to know if this is an Andy Kaufmann routine, because you sabotaged that interview. Please, I need to know."

"No, it's not Andy Kaufmann."

I didn't know what I was dealing with here or even who I was dealing with. If Andy Kaufmann didn't channel himself into Andrew, than surely, Andrew Baumhor has a little of Andy in him. I can't figure this thing out. Not even Dr. Brody can.

If you're interested in making money, concerned about money, interested in earning a living supporting yourself as a rookie sportscaster, forget it, you can earn more money bartending, working at McDonalds, or doing the team's laundry. And you better have a second job, money in the bank, or a family that is supporting you, unless you want to live as a hobo living off food stamps with a cup in your hand standing at the corner with a sign, "Rookie Sportscaster." You're one step away from being homeless.

The money is so low that some employers first shop around for price, in other words will you take the job at this price? First they gather potential applicants of sportscasters who are willing to work for $900.00 to $1,100.00 a month, and then throw in a bartending job at a local restaurant with whom they have a connection. That's what Matt Richert offered Andrew from NNB-Radio in Astoria, Oregon. When Andrew asked Matt, "Did you listen to my tape?"

"No, I don't listen to tapes until I know the person is interested. This way I don't get disappointed if I hear a good tape," Matt Richert informed Andrew. The job was listed as a part time sports play-by-play announcer for high school. "Must have reliable transportation and able to travel from coast I-5 corridor between Olympia-Portland." Matt informed Andrew that one of the sportscasters in a previous year was hired for an on-air TV position in Portland. How can you move cross country for a thousand bucks a month? Well, at least he threw in the bartending job.

You finally get a job as a sports anchor/reporter. You're on TV. People ask for your autograph in the community. Your dream has come true. You're a salaried employee for WDNN in Dalton, Georgia. You earn $15,000.00 a year as a full-time employee. And you're thrilled. You probably are putting in way more than

40 hours a week, because it's your passion, the job demands it, and you want to get ahead. $15,000.00 a year translates into $288.00 a week. You are earning $7.20 cents an hour for 40 hours, before taxes. This does not include the extra hours you are working. If you started out as a management trainee at McDonald's, you'd be surely making more money. Many sports anchor/reporter television and radio play-by-play jobs in smaller markets for rookies are paying $15,000.00 to $20,000.00 a year. Many radio jobs pay less and give you a commission, placing you out in the field selling advertising, like a huckster. The competition is brutal. You can't even land these low paying jobs. Andrew graduated in 2007. What do you think the sportscasters who graduated in 2004, 2005, and 2006 are doing? Many are trying to get established by going after the same jobs as Andrew.

"There is no salary. We will provide housing and $25.00 per day per diem on the road. We do not broadcast home games. You would have the opportunity to be the PA announcer for home games in which you would make $25.00 per game. We have the opportunity to do a daily 1 hour talk show on the radio and a weekly TV show. To do this, we need to sell the advertising. If we decide to bring you aboard and you feel it is a good fit for you, we would like you to come to Yuma as soon as you could to help sell the advertising for the radio show, broadcast and TV show. You would have the opportunity to make some money in commissions on those sales. We have also kicked around the idea of having this person also be the clubhouse manager. For that you would make $1,000 per month

(3.5months) plus player tips," Jason Matlock from the Yuma Scorpions wrote to Andrew in an email. The Scorpions were in the Golden Baseball League from Yuma, Arizona.

On at least two occasions Andrew spoke with General Manager Jason Matlock and clarified the job of a clubhouse manager. "You do the laundry for the team," Jason said. There could have very well been other responsibilities being the clubhouse manger, besides doing the team's laundry, but either Andrew doesn't remember or he didn't discuss it with Jason. The bottom line is the $3,500.00 for being the Laundry Boy is more than Andrew would earn broadcasting the Yuma Scorpion baseball games. Dr. Brody thought it was demeaning. So what have we here: You mixada ameataball wida twenny fi dolla for broadcasting, throw in twennny fi dolla as the PA announcer, you sell a little advertising, a few bucks in players' tips and then you mixada coupala jock straps, whaddaya got? A baseball broadcaster!

If being the Laundry Boy, and washing the team's jock straps is demeaning as a rookie broadcaster, and you can't find a full-time position as a sportscaster, you take a job that will get you in the ballpark, until the real deal happens. I give Andrew credit. If you can't land a job as a full-time sportscaster, go into the park, get onto the field, take a couple of sniffs of the bladed grass, be part of the sports environment, be a member of the team. If you're not in the park, you ain't got a chance.

After graduating from American University in May of 2007, the job opportunities looking bleak, Andrew accepted a three month summer job, and part of his responsibility was being the Trash Man. He'd walk around the stadium the day after the game with a trash bag and collect oddball things, like paper, hamburger wrappers, dirty napkins, beer bottles, and the like. Also among the collectibles were condom wrappers, bottles with tobacco spit, and diapers. He'd accumulate these treasures one by one, and place them in his trash bag. Andrew would proceed around the stadium, and then enter the ball field. He'd walk into the locker room, through the corridor, making his entrance onto the ball field, where similarly many of the greats traversed before him, the Gehirg's, the Ruth's, the DiMaggio's. And now Andrew Baumhor, not retiring but beginning his career, trudges out to the stadium.

Real players wearing uniforms were on the field stretching, throwing the baseball, and conversing. The bright advertising signs on the outfield fence were glowing from sunbeams. The freshly chalked lines were distinctly marked. The aroma of the outfield grass permeated the air. He marched on, not to be denied, as he approached the softly textured infield dirt, recently watered and raked to perfection. No fans were in the stadium yet, many players were gathered around the dugout. Two coaches approached Andrew and one incredulously asked, "Andrew, what are you doing?"

"I'm the Trash Man."

'There's a drive to deep right center field and it's not coming back Jack. Welcome Chris Swauger. First plate appearance back as a HiTom. Just where he left off last season as he got injured on a walk-off grand slam. He sends one over the right center field fence. A line drive. That baby got out of here in a hurry.

One two pitch to Walker. Slider, ground ball shortstop, Burgess to Poutier for one, to first for two. A six, four, three double play to end the inning. No runs, no hits, no errors, no men left on base. We go to the stretch here in Thomasville..."

In my mind I'm gone to Carolina
Can't you see the sunshine
Can't you just feel the moonshine
Ain't it just like a friend of mine
To hit me from behind
Yes I'm gone to Carolina in my mind (4)

Ladies and gentleman without further adieu, with a heart-warming round of applause, please welcome the Play-by-Play Announcer/Media Relations Director/Trash Man, making his professional debut for the Thomasville HiToms defending champions, 2007 baseball team, Andrew Baumhor.

Andrew agreed to the following terms with the Thomasville HiToms, Coastal Plain League defending champions of Thomasville, North Carolina:

"Position: Media Relations Director/Play-by-Play Announcer
Responsibilities
Media Coordination:
(a) Game Day Notes
(b) Post-Game Release and Communication
(c) Web-Site Administration

(d) Player/Coach Interview Requests

(e) Hometown Newspaper Stories (E-mail player updates to hometown papers)

Play-by-Play Announcer:

Handle all play-by-play duties on the HiToms CPL web-pass broadcasts (28 games)

Marketing Assistant:

(a) Update Web-Site and Facilitate Player Head Shots, Photo Album Pictures

(b) Spearhead e-mail blasts to fans, campers and sponsors

(c) Assist with Player & Tommy the HiTom appearances

HiTom Videos:

Produce In-Stadium HiTom Videos

Game Day Operations:

(a) Assist in stadium pre-game preparations

(b) Supervise Legion Games

Compensation:

(a) $100.00 stipend per month (three month timeframe)

(b) $20.00 per HiToms broadcast (28 games, with the possibility of two additional games)

(c) $15.00 Per Legion game

(d) Housing arrangements"

One day in the HiToms office there was a note posted on the board with chores for employees. Andrew: Pick up the trash around the stadium. Andrew was supposed to do this the day after the game.

Andrew moved in with his host family Debbie and John London. As part of my neurosis, I informed Andrew that if his host family was a problem or was like the Adams Family, not to stay and we will make other arrangements. For a change, I was worried.

da da da dum, snap! snap!
da da da dum, snap! snap!
They're creepy and they're kooky,
Mysterious and spooky,
They're altogether ooky,
The London Family!
Their house is a museum
Where people come to see 'em
They really are a screeee-um
The London Family!
da da da dum, snap! snap!
da da da dum, snap! snap! (5)

Andrew had a wonderful experience living with the Londons. Unlike Andrew's father, they are not kooky and spooky. The London family welcomed Andrew into their home with heartfelt hospitality, compassion, and generosity.

In the community, Andrew was becoming quite the celebrity, as he would go with a player to various sites to promote the HiToms. The HiToms were having a Picnic in the Park promotion. Andrew and fan favorite David Thomas, dressed in his HiTom's uniform, went to a day care to drum up business. These kids were five, seven, maybe eight years old. Andrew gave a speech to the class to try and pump the kids up for the game. At the end of the speech the kids lined up for autographs. Andrew was shocked when the kids began asking him for his autograph.

"Who are you?" asked one six year old girl.

"I'm the broadcaster," replied Andrew.

"Even though you're the broadcaster, can I have your autograph?" Andrew was a star. One kid received Andrew's autograph, sat down in his seat, looked at the autograph and went back in line. Andrew looked at him puzzled. "You signed your autograph but you didn't write your number."

"I don't have a number. I'm not a player. I'm the broadcaster."

"What's a broadcaster do?"

"I announce the games on the Internet so people can listen." The kid began jumping up and down yelling with excitement.

One little girl was quite the interrogator. "Do you have a girlfriend?" she asked.

"Yes," Andrew responded.

"Are you married?"

"No."

"Are you in love?" asked the little girl.

"The questioning is inappropriate," as the teacher put a stop to the questions.

Despite Andrew wearing many hats, and the need for preparation before broadcasting the best possible game, there were distractions. Forty five minutes before one game Andrew was frantically doing last minute research, and preparing for the broadcast when one of the HiToms administrators asked, "Andrew are you busy?"

"Yes, I'm doing some preparation for the game."

"I need you to go out and buy Slushies for the players."

"I'm really busy here with work," Andrew said.

"I need this done." And so it went, the Slushies were more important than the broadcast.

Apparently, the HiToms, and the other teams in the league were not earning much money from the broadcasts on the web. The league office was earning the majority of the money.

"It's all about selling beer," Andrew informed me.

Between the Slushies, the diapers, the bottles with tobacco spit, and the condom wrappers, the kid was still able to produce an amazing play-by-play broadcast with much fan appreciation. "We're Tom Fulton's parents and just wanted to thank you for the great coverage of the HiToms games. We've listened to most games and can say without a doubt your coverage spoiled us. You've done a great job describing the play-by-play and make the game easy to follow. Most of the road games were hard to follow because the announcers didn't do a very good job letting the listeners know what was going on. Thanks for the excellent coverage and enthusiasm during the games. Loved the interviews with the players and coaches."

"Scott and I would like to thank you so much for making listening to the web casts so enjoyable. We can honestly say that none of the other sites offer the entertainment that you do. Between listening to you talking about the boys and your interviews with them (we still are laughing at Bill and Patrick, they're nuts you know) it's just been great! Thank you again for making us feel as if we are there even though we're in Georgia! Hope to see and maybe meet you in Florence. Scott and Cynthia Thomas."

"First pitch to Arcadia, high, ball one. 1 and 0 the count to Ryan Arcadia from Villanova. He's from the state of New Jersey. 1 – 0 pitch from Wrenn. Fouls it off behind home plate. 1 and 1 the count to Arcadia. 20 for 26 in stolen bases this past spring for Villanova. One of the top stolen base threats in the Big East. Fouls it off behind home plate again. 1 and 2, falls behind to Wrenn. According to the scouting report on him, he's a great situational hitter, is Arcadia. He can hit and run. He can mark where he wants to hit it, if he wants to go opposite field, if he wants to pull it. From the stretch, 1 – 2 delivery from Wrenn. Curve ball, ground ball right back to Wrenn. Gets it in his glove. Underhand toss to Roller. And he's safe. Can you believe it! Arcadia is safe."

Recap after call: "It was a dribbler back to Wrenn and he got too lackadaisical. He fielded the ball, took a couple of steps off the mound, and gave an underhand toss to Roller at first. But it was a lollipop underhand toss like he was at an Easter Egg Hunt doing a little egg tossing, not wanting to break the baseball egg. And somehow Arcadia beat it out. Back to back infield hits for the Pilots."

During the HiToms season, Andrew and I created another radio demo with play-by-play, highlights, and an interview Andrew did with HiToms pitcher Kevin Jones. Andrew and I were fascinated with this interview. It was so complex you had to listen over and over again to understand the nuances:

Andrew: "With HiToms Pitcher Kevin Jones. We're about 10 to 15 minutes before game time. Every home game I see you right outside your dugout and you play this little flip game with a couple other players. What's that about? What's it called? What's the deal?"

Kevin: "At Old Miss we call it 2 Ball, but at UNC Charlotte and a couple other places they call it Speed Ball. And what it is, everyone has one ball in the circle and one person has two balls, and the main key is you have to have one ball, but you can never have two balls at the same time. You can never have no balls. I mean it gets intense."

Costello: "You gonna be the coach too?"
Abbott: "Yes."
Costello: "And you don't know the fellows' names?"
Abbott: "Well I should."
Costello: "Well then who's on first?"
Abbott: "Yes."
Costello: "I mean the fellow's name."
Abbott: "Who."
Costello: "The first baseman."
Abbott: "Who."
Costello: "The guy playing....."
Abbott: "Who is on first!"
Costello: "I'm asking YOU who's on first."
Abbott: "That's the man's name."
Costello: "That's who's name?"
Abbott: "Yes."
Costello: "Well go ahead and tell me."
Abbott: "That's it."
Costello: "That's who?"
Abbott: "Yes."
Andrew: "So how many players play at one time?"

Kevin: "Today we only had 3 or 4, but yesterday we had like 15. It can be anywhere from the whole team to 2 people."

Andrew: "Let me get this straight. You can't have a ball in your hand?"

Kevin: "You have to have one ball in your hand, but you can't have two."

Andrew: "So when there was 15 people going at once how many balls were flying at once, 15?"

Kevin: "Only one ball can fly at the same time. You have one coming in and one going out. And if somebody else throws it they have no balls. They get a count. You can play up to 4. You can play up to 3. Whatever you have time for."

Costello: "Look, you gotta first baseman?"

Abbott: "Certainly."

Costello: "Who's playing first?"

Abbott: "That's right."

Costello: "When you pay off the first baseman every month, who gets the money?"

Abbott: "Every dollar of it."

Costello: "All I'm trying to find out is the fellow's name on first base."

Abbott: "Who."

Costello: "The guy that gets….."

Abbott: "That's it"

Costello: "Who gets the money….."

Abbott: "He does, every dollar. Sometimes his wife comes down and collects it."

Costello: "Whose wife?"

Abbott: "Yes, what's wrong with that?"

Costello: "Look, all I wanna know is when you sign up the first baseman, how does he sign his name?"
Abbott: "Who."
Costello: "The guy."
Abbott: "Who."
Costello: "How does he sign...."
Abbott: "That's how he signs it."
Costello: "Who?"
Abbott: "Yes."
Costello: "All I'm trying to find out is what's the guy's name on first base."
Abbott: "No. What is on second base."
Costello "I'm not asking you who's on second."
Abbott: "Who's on first."(6)
Andrew: "How important is this for you guys? Obviously it keeps you loose before the game."
Kevin: It's just a game. But it keeps our competitive mentality trying to get us not focused for the game, but just get the competitor back out in front of us before the game."
Andrew: "How competitive does it get?"
Kevin: "Oh it gets crazy. People make enemies. All of us are friends. But when you get there you have no friends, just all enemies, all competitors."
Andrew received a magnificent recommendation letter at the end of the season:
"Prospective Employer,
In the summer of 2007, the HiToms Baseball organization had the privilege of having Andrew Baumhor serve as its lead broadcaster.
Accepting the challenge of play-by-play announcer with an air of confidence and enthusiasm, Mr. Baum-

hor quickly established his proficiency as a broadcaster and dependable employee. Capturing the excitement of Finch Field through extensive pre-game research and personal interaction with our loyal fan base, Andrew asserted himself as the league's best announcer with his descriptive calls, insightful game analysis and enlightening player/coach interviews.

Professionally prepared for each contest, Andrew displayed his range of excellence by citing statistics from both collegiate and Coastal Plain League seasons and interjecting opposing player scouting reports from the HiToms coaching staff.

Approaching each broadcast as if performing on a national stage, Baumhor's passionate tone uniquely captures the vitality and tranquility of our wonderful sport.

It is my opinion that Andrew Baumhor possesses the physical and mental makeup to excel as a professional sports broadcaster. His experience and proficiency will surely light the way for thousands of fans to enjoy their team's pitch-by-pitch or play-by-play.

Please feel free to contact me if you have any questions about Andrew and good luck.

Regards, Greg Suire, HiToms President"

The Coastal Plain League monitored and listened to the various teams' broadcasters and knew exactly what they were doing when they asked Andrew to broadcast the Petitt Cup playoffs. The Coastal Plain League wanted a true artist, they wanted the real deal, they wanted Pablo Picasso.

"1 – 0 pitch, delivery. Thomas is bunting down the third base line. It's a beauty, it's gonna be a single.

They're trying to make the ball go foul. Burgess to third. Safe! The third baseman, Brock Sutton was standing about 10 feet up the line from home plate watching like when you go to Europe and observe the beautiful art work from Pablo Picasso and Monet. He was staring at the beautiful bunt from David Thomas, blowing at it hoping it would go foul. Instead it stayed right inside the line. Meanwhile, Burgess, who's busting down to second base makes the turn. There's no one covering third. Burgess slides in safely. Runners at the corners with no one out and the momentum has swung back to Thomasville!"

As the artist continued his calls for the HiToms, the Coastal Plain League emailed Andrew an offer to broadcast the playoffs. The league has two announcers for the playoffs, an automatic bid for the announcer where the playoffs are played, and to the best broadcaster in the league who happened to be Andrew. But when you're dealing with an artist, they're very temperamental, eccentric and often beat to a different drummer. I was so proud of Andrew. What an unbelievable opportunity, not to mention the HiToms were seeking back-to-back championships. It was possible Andrew could be the broadcaster for the HiToms playing for the championship. What a way to cap off an incredible season. Not so fast, please, let's not pressure the artist. I mean after all, we're up to 400 resume packages with no full-time job. He could be busy. Maybe he's performing other art. Who knows what's in the minds of these geniuses? Perhaps the shadow. The first offer was for no money, but a hotel room and food at the ballpark. Andrew would have to pay traveling expenses, an hour and a half drive. The artist rejected the first offer. The second offer included $100.00. The artist rejected the offer and countered with $150.00. The Coastal Plain League hired another sportscaster for the playoffs. Perhaps Andrew should have hired Drew Rosenhaus to negotiate.

On February 28, 2007, Andrew boarded a plane in Washington D.C., for an interview on March 1 with the hopes of landing a job at ESPN as a Production Assistant. He had an interview with Fred Brown in Bristol, Connecticut. Mr. Brown is the Director of Production Recruitment and Talent Negotiations. We sent 9 resume packages to ESPN, but not one directly to Fred Brown. However, John Skipper forwarded Andrew's resume package to Al Jaffe who is VP of Production Recruitment & Talent Negotiations who apparently forwarded it to Fred Brown. Also involved in this process was Denise Pellegrini who works with John Skipper and Susan Landry who works with Fred Brown. If all this seems confusing, perhaps it is, but Scott Reiss' theory from ESPN "of six degrees of separation" is that we are all six contacts away from the person doing the hiring and that's apparently what happened with Andrew's resume package.

Fred Brown took Andrew on a tour of the facility, walking Andrew through the SportsCenter studio, and another studio used for multiple shows, like Baseball Tonight and NFL Live. Fred interviewed Andrew in a private room and began bombarding him with sports questions, and then left Andrew in the room alone for ten minutes to come up with an on-air topical sports story to pitch to the producer.

"In the NFL Scouting Combine, I don't think the Wonderlic test should be used to evaluate players. Because last year Vince Young received one of the worst scores ever and he was Offensive Rookie of the Year. He may have lost millions of dollars, because he got drafted lower as a result of a bad performance on the Wonderlic test. And other players may be loosing money from low scores on the Wonderlic test. For my story, I would compare NFL players who took the Wonderlic test and see how they are performing in the NFL. Is there a correlation between doing well on the Wonderlic test and a player's performance in the NFL," Andrew stated.

This got me wondering about this Wonderlic test. Here's a few questions from the Wonderlic test:

1. "How many of the five pairs of items below are exact duplicates?"
Nieman, K.M./Neiman, K.M.
Thomas, G.K/Thomas, C.K.
Hoff, J.P./Hoff, J.P.
Pino, L.R./Pina, L.R.
Warner, T.S./Wanner, T.S.

2. "A train travels 20 feet in 1/5 second. At this same speed, how many feet will it travel in three seconds?"

Let me know if I'm crazy, but who the fuck cares how fast the train is coming? I'd be worried about how fast the 300 pound linebacker is coming with the desire to knock the shit out of me.

3. "Assume the first 2 statements are true. Is the final one: a) true, b) false, c) not certain?"
The boy plays baseball. All baseball players wear hats. The boy wears a hat.

4. "Three individuals form a partnership and agree to divide the profits equally. X invests $9,000, Y invests $7,000, Z invests $4,000. If the profits are $4,800, how much less does X receive than if the profits were divided in proportion to the amount invested?"

I'd like to take the schmuck who made the Wonderlic test mandatory and put him out on the football field with some linebackers, then we'll see what type of Wonderlic he is.

On August 16, 2007, the call came in from ESPN to Andrew. At 10:35 A.M. eastern time, Susan Landry offered Andrew a full time position at ESPN, 11 months after the first resume package was mailed.

There you have it, that's our story of a never ending saga of a dream to become a sportscaster. Before I leave, I have a message for you big shots at ESPN. If you happen to pass a small kid in the hall with curly hair from Philadelphia, please be nice to him, he's my son, Andrew Baumhor, the greatest sportscaster in the world!